Acclaim

"From theatre in London's West End, to Broadway, and Hollywood's nascent enterprise of moving pictures, *Shades of Neverland* takes you on a journey of faith, trust, and pixie dust past the second star to the right and straight on till happily ever after. *Shades of Neverland* is the continuation of Peter Pan's story that my heart needed!"

—LORIE LANGDON, bestselling author of Disney Villains' Happily Never After series

"A stunning recollection of a past age, a continuation of a best-loved story, and the finding of oneself in the memories of childhood. This is a beautiful, beautiful story that simply must be savored."

—AJ SKELLY, bestselling author of The Wolves of Rock Falls series and Magik Prep Academy series

"As atmospheric as a windswept painting, *Shades of Neverland* is a classic retelling with lovely dashes of nostalgia, wit, and good old-fashioned pining. I was charmed from the first page until the picture-perfect happy ending."

—BRITTANY EDEN, bestselling author of the Heartbooks series

Shades of Neverland

Quill & Flame
PUBLISHING HOUSE

Shades of Neverland

Shades of Neverland

Quill & Flame
PUBLISHING HOUSE

CAREY CORP

In memory of Mary Corp who has gone on to her next awfully big
adventure.

The universe is made up of stories, not atoms.
-Muriel Rukeyser

In the back...

This book contains a discussion guide for classrooms and book clubs at the back.

Author's Note

Shades of Neverland is a whimsical continuation of J.M. Barrie's beloved tale, weaving characters and imagery from the original novel *Peter and Wendy* into an entirely new story. Set in early 20th century London and America, the story is interwoven with historical people and places connected to J.M. Barrie's original play and world.

This is a deceptively simple, all too common story about lost selves. We grow up and cease to be certain of our way. We become lost. It is a gradual process, so that we cannot even be certain when the loss occurred, only that we have misplaced something vital to our lives. Like marbles, ribbons, and our last pinch of pixie dust, we have put away childish things, and in doing so, misplaced the best part of ourselves. Years later, we wonder where our youth, indeed our very lives, have gone. Only when we reconnect with our lost child can we live the vibrant, passionate life that calls to us in our dreams.

Preface

For the moment, she had forgotten his ignorance about kisses.

"I thought you would want it back," he said bitterly, and offered to return her the thimble.

"Oh dear," said the nice Wendy, "I don't mean a kiss, I mean a thimble."

"What's that?"

"It's like this." She kissed him.

"Funny!" said Peter gravely. "Now shall I give you a thimble?"

"If you wish to," said Wendy, keeping her head erect this time.

Peter thimbled her...

Come Away, Come Away!

Peter Pan

J.M.Barrie

The Night of the Thimble

London Town 1907

All children grow up. Wendy Moira Angela Darling was no exception.

She promised herself she would never forget what it was like to be a child, but being still young, she could not foresee the toll that growing up would have on her. The way it happened was this.

It started the night she left the nursery for good on the eve of her thirteenth birthday. Thirteen, of course, is the beginning of the end. At first, she returned each evening to recount to her brothers the stories of their grand adventures in the Neverlands. Over time, however, she came to the boys less and less frequently. When the boys were sent away to school, she stopped telling stories altogether.

Peter, I am most sorry to report, was witness to it all. In the shadows outside her window, as faithful as the chiming of Big Ben, Peter watched as his Wendy Darling put away her childhood dreams one by one. Lately, he wondered if she could recall even the slightest detail about the Neverland or himself. If the name Peter Pan were mentioned to her in passing, would it have any effect? Could the thought of an eternal boy still stir the girlhood in one so nearly a woman? Peter felt sure he would soon be no more to her than a little dust in the box in which she kept her toys.

Weighted by a profound sense of loss, Peter flew through the midnight London skies. Tonight, he was to have his last glimpse of his—*Wendy*. Being yet a boy, he had no other name to describe what she was to him. She was his other half, his very own and dearest. For as long as he lived, he would never have another Wendy.

On the morrow, she would be sixteen...and a woman. So it was time, Peter decided, to abandon her to adulthood. Tomorrow, he would forget.

Engaged as he was in fortifying his decision to forsake her, Peter almost flew past the Darling house. Accustomed to stealing upon it in full slumber, he nearly failed to recognize the residence awake and ablaze. The change elicited in him an involuntary shiver. It seemed to be a bad omen. He hovered in indecision until the feel of the cool object in his hand recalled him to his purpose. *A kiss.* If he were never to see his Wendy again, he would not leave until he had given her a final kiss.

He alighted to her windowsill cautiously. The brightly lit room was empty—another first for the boy and it vexed him. Previously, he had never been denied the object of his visits. Lit by softly glowing moonlight, his Wendy had always been accessible to him. His cocky nature, furthermore, led him to believe it would always be so.

Puzzled, Peter descended into the garden below. Deep in shadow, he peered through the great French doors at a bustle of activity and finery.

A party!

With growing fascination, the boy watched a dozen or so young men twirl their partners across the polished walnut floor. In the hall beyond, there seemed to be a banquet table and even more people making merry. Such activity made the wary Peter anxious to depart, but he would not, indeed could not, leave until he had satisfied the purpose of his mission. He squared his chin in resolve; he would not go until Wendy had received his gift.

Peter did not have to look far for that which he sought. In fact, without his knowing, she had been in his sight the entire time. As he watched the dancers, a young lady in a shimmering pink gown drew his eye.

Observing her first from behind, he followed the form of her dress up to her bare shoulders. He traced her slender neck to a mass of honey blonde curls worn high on her head in the fashion of the day. She wore pearls on her earlobes and her hair was adorned with tiny pink rosebuds. As the fine lady turned around, he noticed her high brow, the deep blush in her cheeks, and her full red lips half open in a laugh.

Despite her remarkable beauty, she meant no more to Peter than any other partygoer. It was not until she had completed her turn and the boy was able to regard her eyes that he knew her.

For the third time that night, the boy was confounded by the unexpected. Could that stranger in pink really be his own, true Wendy? For some unknown reason he had the urge to laugh at the absurdity of her costume. Instead, but equally as inexplicable, the boy developed a lump in his throat and his eyes commenced to produce great tears that rolled down his boyish cheeks.

To Peter's surprise, the creature in pink crossed the room to the very window behind which he was spying. Had she seen him? Was she coming to explain to him the circumstances that caused her to be almost unrecognizable? The boy shrank back into the darkness even as the door opened in front of him. There was a momentary rush of music before the young lady shut the door and crossed out into the quiet of the garden.

Peter held his breath as she took a few steps across the courtyard and then turned to seat herself on the garden bench. Her cerulean eyes met his across the darkness, as she fixed her gaze on the exact spot where he was hiding. Not daring to move, he waited for her to address him.

Instead, Wendy's gaze shifted dreamily to the stars and she sighed to herself.

Peter's mouth opened in disbelief. Was it possible? Did she really not know he was there? If truly ignorant of his presence, could she not feel him so near? That moment confirmed the boy's worst fears. His Wendy had forgotten him. Therefore, it was time to say goodbye. He would give her his kiss and then go.

Before the boy could move from the shadows, music once again imposed on the stillness of the garden. A smartly-dressed young man passed through the door and approached the bench. Peter, his stomach beginning to ache, shrank back further into the darkness, all the while never taking his eyes off the youth who was now seating himself on Wendy's bench.

The youth was pale and delicate looking, appearing more female than male. Peter felt certain he could take him in a duel. During his time in the Neverlands, he had bested many a blackguard. Next to that unsavory lot, the youth would be an easy conquest.

Poor Peter. Being still a boy, he had not yet learned there were many ways to best one's opponent and that violence rarely worked in competitions of the heart.

All the while looking on, he watched as the youth took Wendy's hand in his and said something to her in low tones. A light musical laugh escaped from her lips. The boy crept closer straining to hear.

"I do not know where they come from," said Wendy. "I just know that I have received one as a gift every birthday for the past three years."

"A secret admirer?" inquired the youth. Wendy smiled, a most beautiful smile, and turned to face him.

"When I was still a girl I used to think they were birthday gifts from the fairies." She nearly added that she did not believe in fairies but some unnamed superstition had always kept her from uttering those words.

Inching closer, Peter's hand tightened on the gift clutched within.

"And now, Miss Darling," proclaimed the youth. "I have a gift for you that I hope you will find equaling as pleasing." With that, the young man placed his free hand upon Wendy's cheek and, leaning in close, preceded to give her—*a thimble!*

Peter watched the thimble with horror. His chest convulsed and his hands clenched into fists until the item in his grasp broke in two. Of their own volition, his feet propelled him across the little garden until he was nearly upon the couple; but since they both had their eyes closed, he remained unseen. Wendy opened her eyes first and gasped. In the same instant, the boy took off like a rocket into the starry London sky.

Wendy leapt up causing the youth to do the same. Alarmed by her abrupt behavior, he put his hand on her shoulder, demanding, "What's happened, Miss Darling?"

"A boy," she replied, stepping into the courtyard and looking wildly about. "I thought I saw a boy."

The youth looked about the deserted garden and then took her trembling hand in his, assuring her in gentle tones, "There's no one here, dearest."

Feeling slightly foolish, Wendy looked down. And fortunate for her that she did so, because at her feet appeared to be a ragged bit of glass or shell. Whatever the tiny object was, it certainly had not been there moments ago. To get a better look, she bent down and retrieved the item with an unsteady hand. Examining it in the moonlight, she realized she held half of a beautiful porcelain thimble. The damaged trinket had appeared as magically as the boy had vanished.

Peter hurled himself through the air above Wendy's house. His entire body knotted with emotions for which he had no words. He clenched his fists, his sharp nails creating little half-moons in the tender flesh of his palms. Blinking rapidly against the wind and the sudden wet stinging in his eyes, he flew higher and higher.

A sob wretched itself free of his throat, but whether born of anger or sorrow he could not say. He wanted to cry, scream, and fight all at the same time. He wanted to hurt Wendy and to save her. Most of all he knew beyond certainty that he could never forsake her and that he would surely die if she belonged to another!

In that instant, Peter Pan felt himself begin to grow up. Then he began to fall...

2

The Morning After the Party

The boy!

Wendy Darling awoke with a start. She flew to the open window to search for some sign of his presence. The sun was not yet visible overhead, and the house remained heavy in slumber due to the past evening's frivolity. She leaned forward straining to peer over the garden wall. There was some commotion in the next street over, which, despite her best efforts, remained hidden from view. A thorough scan of the skies yielded nothing further except a few fading stars in the West.

"It was just a dream," she murmured to herself. But in truth, these were the shades of Neverland, which persist after we've lost our way to remind us of what once was.

Returning to her bed, she mused over the strange visions that troubled her sleep. She recalled beautiful mermaids, fierce Indians, and magnificent swordfights. There was a terrible pirate with a hook for a hand—and her brothers were there. She'd been forced to walk the plank at knifepoint. Shivering, she remembered the horror of falling—then not falling—flying!

She'd been flying—and not alone. There was a boy, strong and sure and brave. Moreover, he had saved her from certain death. He came to her often in her dreams and at his side, she had the grandest of adventures. Last night, she had given him a kiss—no not a kiss, exactly—a thimble. In the world of the boy, a thimble was called a kiss and a kiss called a thimble. The recollection made Wendy smile. She willed herself to conjure up the image of the boy but the more she concentrated the more elusive he became, like the morning mist.

After a moment, she shook her head. How foolish she was being. Clearly, the events of the previous night had been the basis for her strange dream—James's kiss in the garden, the boy who vanished into thin air, the little thimble.

The thimble! Wendy jumped out of bed and hurried to her dressing table. Reverently, she pulled a small box out of the drawer. The box was black and glossy with beautiful exotic markings. It had been a gift from the orient given to her by her father, and it kept her dearest treasures. She set the box on the table as if suddenly afraid to open it. Still trying to sort out dream from reality, she was unsure what she would find within.

Almost reverently, Wendy lifted the top. Nestled among cards, ribbons, and pressed flowers was a little collection of thimbles. The first was golden and had appeared on her windowsill without explanation on the morning of her thirteenth birthday. For her fourteenth, shiny silver, followed by deep copper on her fifteenth—both left to be found in the same mysterious way. And yes, next to them the object which she sought, half a porcelain thimble.

Wendy picked up the trinket and felt its coolness between her fingers. It was exquisite, creamy white with tiny hand painted pink roses. *Where is the other half?* she wondered. She pressed the delicate porcelain to her cheek. Closing her eyes, she meditated on its smoothness, its coolness. She carefully ran a finger along the break as if trying to memorize every detail of its ragged edges. Somehow, she felt sure that her fate, even her very life, depended on this thimble. Only when the other piece was found and the two halves restored to wholeness would the true course of her life be revealed to her.

From somewhere deep below, the muted clank of a pot signaled the house beginning to stir. Reluctantly, Wendy put the broken thimble back into the box and the box into the drawer. It would not do to be in her nightdress when Aunt Mildred called for her. She needed to be properly attired and looking every bit the grown woman her family expected her to be...even if that woman was an elusive stranger.

Today, she turned sixteen, yet she felt no different than the she had last week or last year. She felt trapped in a curious limbo between selves, no longer the child that once inhabited the family nursery, nor fully the young woman who'd just been introduced into London society. What Wendy didn't realize is the magic of her youth was already slipping away, and in her haste to grow up, she had already begun to lose the best part of herself.

Ringing for Liza, she admonished herself for indulging in girlish fantasies. *Enough*, she chided. *Today, I am grown.* Still, before dressing, she could not help but take one last look out the window and into the morning sky for the figure of a flying boy.

One street over, Peter awakened to a sharp, persistent rapping against his right shoulder. In a state of deep sleep, his head swirled with disturbing visions; the specifics of which, he was unable to recall, but whose shades would cling to the edges of his consciousness like spider webs filled him with vague apprehension.

The first thing he felt upon waking was the cold, then the dampness. Gradually, he became aware of various aches and pains, unfamiliar sensations caused in part by sleeping in a doorway. He was possessed by an overall trepidation, and in the pit of his stomach lodged a tight ball of fear. Try as he might, the boy could never recall feeling such a lack of arrogance about himself or his circumstances. The experience was foreign and uncomfortable, like wearing new shoes.

Disoriented, he rolled over to find two men regarding him with a mixture of concern and distrust. One, undoubtedly the source of the tapping, wore the uniform of an officer of the law and clutched a nightstick. The other was clearly a businessman. Both men had come upon Peter at the same time from opposite directions, and each had his own reasons for rousting the sleeping boy. For the former, it was obligation to his duty and for the latter, obligation to his doorstep.

"You boy," demanded the constable. "What are you doing there?"

"I don't know, Sir," replied the boy in earnest.

Leveling his nightstick at the boy's chest just under his chin and raising it steadily produced the practiced effect of forcing the boy to his feet. "Where do you come from?"

"I do not know, Sir," repeated the boy looking from one man to the other.

The businessman, a kind and gentle old soul, bent down and inquired of him, "Lad, where are your parents?"

"In truth, I have none," answered the boy. Although he could not offer why, he knew this to be true with a certainty that bordered on insolence.

Upon hearing the boy's reply, the constable pushed forward. "An orphan is it? Well, back to the orphanage with you!" You see, the officer, who possessed no patience for vagabonds or children, had been looking for a reason to seize the boy.

The businessman, however, harbored more progressive ideas concerning the young citizen. Noting the child's growing concern, he inserted himself between the zealous officer and the lad. "How old are you boy?" he inquired.

Peter's age was another certainty for which he had no evidence except the arrogance of his heart. "Today, I am grown. Sir."

While the answer was far from satisfactory, the kindly old man seemed obliged to let it go. "And have you really no one?"

The boy shook his head. "I am alone in the world, Sir."

Again, the constable endeavored to grab the boy.

The old man foiled this attempt by deftly intercepting the officer's hand with his own and giving it a vigorous shake. "Sir, I thank you for your diligence." He let the hand drop. "I do not presume to know about you, but I believe in providence. The boy is quite alone, and I have need of another apprentice. He is of age, and I therefore propose to remove him from my doorstep by bringing him into my business. We certainly wish to trouble you no further."

The constable did not budge but rather scrutinized the boy as if hoping to find the slightest provocation to haul him away.

The old man, giving no heed to the officer, turned back to the boy and placed a fatherly and protective hand on his shoulder. "What say you, my fine lad? Would you like to come and work for me in my *office*?"

At the mention of the word *office,* Peter shuddered. He did not know why the word offended him so. However, not wishing to disoblige the generosity of the speaker and having no other prospects, he answered with a slight nod.

"Very good," said the businessman, as he produced a key and inserted it into the lock behind the boy. "If you are to be my apprentice, I think I should know what to call you?"

"Peter," replied the boy.

"And your surname?"

"I have none, Sir."

Frowning, the man hesitated. For a moment, Peter thought his would-be benefactor had changed his mind and was about to deliver him to the still-waiting constable. With growing anxiety, Peter watched the frown of the old man break into a jolly smile.

"Well, Peter, if you have no surname of your own, then I suppose I shall just have to give you mine."

With that, the pair entered the old man's business, leaving the astonished constable mouth open in the street. And that is how Peter of Neverland became Peter Smythe of Smythe and Sons Accounting Firm of Highbury Street.

3

The Boy in the Park

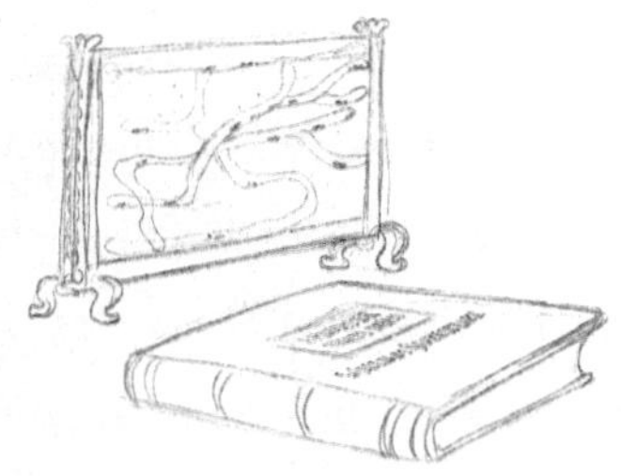

Peter learned that Sir William Smythe of Smythe and Sons had, in fact, no sons of his own. He was, rather, the younger of the two original sons and had inherited the business from his father. Being the sole Smythe survivor, and also a widower, Sir William had reconciled to himself the reality that he would eventually have to sell his family business. Then, one day, while in Kensington Gardens, he struck up a conversation with an orphaned lad who was willing to work for food. Sir William, both observant and fatherly, saw beneath the boy's grime, the spark of intelligence and reason. As he had with Peter, he took the boy in that very hour calling him apprentice and son. That is how Peter came to make the acquaintance of Griffin Smythe, adopted son of Sir William Smythe.

About twenty minutes after the confounded constable had been abandoned in the street, Griffin Smythe, a dark lad of nearly seventeen, came hurrying into the office carrying a stack of files. Upon seeing Sir William and Peter, Griffin dropped his files to the floor and smartly saluted the latter as "Sir." Griffin could not explain why it felt natural and right to do so any more than Peter could explain why it felt right to be greeted as such.

Sir William, assuming the salutation was for him, put an aged hand on his adopted son's shoulder. "Griffin, my son."

"Aye, father?"

"Soon you shall be a clerk, and we shall have need of an apprentice."

"I suppose so father."

"This is Peter," the old man continued. "He is quite alone in the world and has need of some position. It is my intent to give him one. Tell me, my son, what would you say to having a brother?"

For one brief moment, Peter wondered how the only heir to Sir William's estate and the sole possessor of the man's affections would feel having to split his good fortune with another. Griffin, however, was a kind soul, as incapable of jealousy as malice or murder. Smiling from ear to ear, he clasped Peter in a brotherly bear hug exclaiming, "It is my dearest wish to have a brother!"

Therefore, in a single morning Peter gained a surname, an occupation, a residence, a father, and a brother. The only thing the boy had wont of was a mother, but the idea never even occurred to him.

Things that would trouble others terribly did not seem to bother Peter Smythe. For example, he was not bothered that he did not have a mother or that he didn't know A from Z. He was not concerned when his teeth began to fall out and, when on every evening for about a month, he would lose a tooth only to wake up in the morning to find an even larger one had taken its place.

In the way some children seem to do when no one is watching, Peter seemed to age three years overnight. In just a few months, he stood taller than both his new father and brother. He was, you see, making up for lost time.

Although he could remember some details about himself with perfect certainty, he could not recall his life before the doorstep of Smythe and Sons. And while this would put some into a terror, Peter felt it was of little consequence. Convinced the puzzle of his existence would be solved in the future, looking back seemed to him a fruitless waste of energy.

With such purpose, Peter accomplished in one year what other young men took a boyhood to master. Under the patient tutelage of Sir William, Peter learned not only the basics of education but also languages, art, and his personal favorite, literature. Peter, whose spirit was ever restless for adventure, found kindred souls in the characters of Chaucer, Dante, and Shakespeare.

Griffin, preferring math and science to prose, bore his brother's fascinations with patience. Though Peter was younger in age, Griffin idolized him for his confidence and passion. It could be said that the brothers challenged each other in the best of ways. Peter propelled Griffin into grand adventures and benign mischief. Griffin, in turn, tempered his brother's impulsiveness, teaching him to think things through and to proceed with patience.

When not in the office or in lessons with Father, the brothers would retreat to their most favorite place on earth, Kensington Gardens. For hours, they would lie in the grass, reading aloud a new book or play. Sometimes Peter would demand they act out a scene, usually a great battle or magnificent swordfight. Sometimes Griffin would point out a particular piece of flora or fauna taking opportunity to increase his brother's knowledge of natural science.

On the afternoon in question, Peter was reading *A Midsummer Night's Dream* aloud while Griffin was enjoying the labors of a colony of ants.

"Oh, Griffin," the younger brother exclaimed. "I think I was Puck in another life!"

"I would swear you are Puck now!" retorted the elder.

Peter rose to his feet, hands on his hips in a challenge. "Are you calling me an imp?"

"Aye, an imp, a scoundrel, and a jackanapes!" replied Griffin, breaking into a full run as the last word escaped his lips. Peter, feigning offense, followed after in close pursuit. The brothers chased each other round and round the park at a full gallop, their cries demanding the attention of all within earshot.

Peter, being slightly faster and more cunning, managed to corner Griffin in a grove of trees. Though Griffin was tall for his age, Peter, who had recently surpassed him in height and muscle, clearly had the advantage. "Do you surrender, Sir?"

"Never!" cried the older brother.

"If you surrender, there will be mercy for you," Peter countered.

"Death first!" came the reply.

"Very well, you have been warned, and now you will die!" Then Peter, whose nature was never to be merciful with victory in reach, did something quite astounding. He walked away.

At first Griffin thought it was a trick, some ploy to lull him into a false sense of confidence before striking the fatal blow. However, a closer look at Peter's now pale face convinced Griffin that their game had been quite forgotten.

Griffin hurried to his brother's side. "Peter what is the matter?"

"Oh Griffin!" Peter pointed. "There! Do you see?"

Griffin's eyes followed Peter's outstretched hand to the opposite end of the garden. At first, he saw nothing unusual, just a typical assortment of people enjoying the fine weather, but then near the ground—small movements. Straining, he could barely believe what he was seeing. "Peter, what is that? Is that a—a baby?"

"He fell out of his pram while his nurse was looking the other way!"

"I do not see a nurse."

"There." He pointed in another direction, "She has nearly reached the street." Then Peter began to run toward the opposite end of the garden. Over his shoulder he barked, "Griffin you must stop that nurse!"

With instant obedience, Griffin followed his brother's command. While he went after the oblivious nurse, Peter gathered up the child and cradled him to his heart.

"There, there my lad," he crowed. "You shall not be without a mother tonight. Peter will save you."

By this time, Griffin had retrieved the oblivious nursemaid. Made crosser by her obvious negligence, she snatched the child from Peter's arms without as much as a word of thanks. Peter did not doubt by the time she got her young charge home, that in self-preservation, her own mind would greatly alter her version of events. With great trembling and emotion, she would recount for her employers how she alone had saved her precious cargo from a vile gang of ruffians. Still, Peter took consolation in the knowledge that despite the facts of the story, the babe's mother would hold him a little tighter and longer for many evenings to come.

Griffin, while not fully understanding, sensed how deeply the events that had just unfolded affected his brother. So, taking him by the arm, the older brother led the younger one home.

That evening in Peter's dreams, baby after baby fell out of his pram. Try as he might, Peter could not save them all. Their oblivious nurses were leaving them behind. The little lads were being lost...

Wendy Darling preferred the company of females to males. Being pretty and of good family, she had no end of would be-suitors, but Wendy found the opposite sex, on the whole, tiresome. She was at that awkward age where boy and girls, having stopped playing together, had not yet learned to communicate. Males certainly seemed to speak another language. When talking to a young man, she had to work at conversation. She would coax him into talking about himself with artful questions then appear to listen carefully to his dull replies.

"Conversation is an art." Her Aunt Mildred never failed to remind her. "It is the duty of a wife to draw her husband out. Who knows what opportunity will become evident through artful conversation?"

In a most regal and authoritative manner, the spinster would instruct her, "You must always be vigilant, Wendy, to seize opportunities for your husband's advancement. A carefully worded card, a chance meeting in the right shops, a deliberately chosen charity, an invitation to an exclusive party, a coy response to your husband's employer, a perceptive compliment to the employer's wife—these can all progress and secure your husband's position. While it is the husband that earns the living it is the wife who determines the family's status."

Under Aunt Mildred's scrupulous tutelage, Wendy practiced the art of conversation weekly. Indeed, talking to young men made her head ache!

With her girlfriends, however, Wendy found that conversation was like breathing; it was natural and effortless, flowing rhythmically without self-consciousness or contrivance. They spoke the same language and understood each other's passions. Yes, Wendy greatly preferred spending afternoons in the company of her female friends.

On the afternoon in question, Wendy was taking in the lovely spring air with her best and dearest friend Margaret Daphne Sharpe, whom everyone called Maimie. Admired for her mass of flowing red curls, Maimie was considered a beauty only slightly diminished by her wit and outspokenness. Strolling through Kensington Gardens arm in arm, the girls were discussing the one subject that had had a monopoly on their conversations of late—young men.

"I am just saying that James is a young man worthy of *esteem*," baited Maimie, a smile playing about the corners of her full mouth.

"Oh, rubbish!" retorted Wendy. Then in a perfectly ghastly imitation of Aunt Mildred, she continued, "James Christopher Whitby III is the embodiment of good breeding. That coupled with his good form make him quite a desirable catch. Indeed, if I were but a few years younger, I should snatch him up myself." To emphasize her point, she turned to Maimie, making horrid kissing sounds.

Maimie joined in the game with her own imitation of the spinster. "It certainly does not hurt that his father owns the largest bank in London. A more desirable match in all of England, there cannot be."

"Aunt Mildred can have him," Wendy said in earnest. "I used to think because he was quiet that he was pensive. I was mistaken. He simply has nothing to say."

"He is rich," her friend countered.

"He is boring!"

"He is handsome."

"But only in so much as one without passion can be. He has no fire; no, not even a spark! He is so jolly proper with his good breeding and good family and good form. I say good riddance!"

"He is a *good* match. Your Aunt Mildred constantly says so."

Wendy stopped and pressed her dear friend's hand to her heart.

"Maimie, would you have me wither on the vine like the morning glory in the heat of the day? For that is what will surely happen if I am forced to marry James Whitby!"

Maimie kissed her friend penitently. "Of course not! But what is to become of my Wendy? Shall she become a spinster like Aunt Mildred?"

Wendy shivered. "I cannot abide that either. I have always wanted to become a mother with babes at my knee." A sudden smile played on her lips. "Perhaps, I will become a novelist."

"A novelist!" replied the redhead with delicious enjoyment. "What a scandal!"

The girls walked a couple steps in silence musing over the idea.

"Poor Aunt Mildred," said Wendy. Again imitating, she declared, "She could have married James Christopher Whitby, heir to the largest bank in all Britannia. She could have been the cream of society. Now look at her—a novelist! Oh, my heart will not bear it!" The friends erupted into fits of giggles.

When both girls had sufficiently calmed, Maimie uttered most sympathetically, "Poor Aunt Mildred," starting their fits anew. It might have gone on like that all afternoon if the wind had not interceded with amusements of its own.

As fate would have it, a gust of wind snatched Maimie's handkerchief from her hand as she was trying in vain to mop up tears of laughter. The merry girl then took off after the cloth, leaving Wendy behind to catch her breath.

As Maimie gave chase to her handkerchief, she nearly collided with a youth, who not only did not pause to retrieve her item but did not even seem to notice her plight. Not accustomed to being overlooked, Maimie was mildly vexed by this.

Handkerchief forgotten, she watched indignantly as the young man hurried across the park. Though he had the height and form of a man, his movement was still rather boyish. The effect was not altogether unpleasant to watch. Even with his back to her, his impression conveyed a distinct handsomeness. With growing fascination, Maimie watched him scoop something up from the ground; she could not see what—an animal perhaps. He was cuddling and cooing to the thing so tenderly that her heart stirred and her eyes welled up with tears.

Presently, a cross looking nurse wheeling a pram came and snatched the thing away. It was a babe! Maimie could not have been more surprised if the youth had flown. In another instant, another young man, this one darker and stockier, took the youth by the arm, led him out of the park and away from sight.

Meanwhile, Wendy had become annoyed at her friend for tarrying so long over a silly handkerchief! Though Maimie hailed from the finest breeding and family, Wendy thought she sometimes lacked the practicality of common sense and planned to scold her thoroughly on her return. As her friend approached, however, something in Maimie's countenance made Wendy stop short.

"Maimie, tell! What is it?"

"A babe," replied the trembling girl. "Fallen from his pram and abandoned by his nurse. Saved by a young man who held the infant so tenderly that my throat lumps to tell of it."

Turning deathly pale, Wendy took off like a shot, running in the direction from which her friend had come. She ran all the way to the park entrance but saw no boy. When her friend caught up to her, Wendy turned on her grasping her shoulders sharply. "Where did he go?"

"He left. Another young man came to fetch him, and they left the park."

But Wendy would not take this for an answer. She dragged the unfortunate girl all over the park, looking for any sign of the youth, but after an hour of searching, all they had to show for their efforts was an abandoned volume of Shakespeare. Exhausted, the girls collapsed on a bench. Even then, Wendy made Maimie miserable in the telling and retelling of her story, prompting her to recall every tiny detail. When she was satisfied that she had collected all the information Maimie was able to give, Wendy sat as still as a stone in contemplative silence.

Maimie, concerned for her dearest friend but fearful to break the quiet lest she be cross-examined again, sat stoically by, waiting. Finally, she could bear it no longer. "Wendy," she ventured. "Are you ill? You are so pale and grave. Do tell what the matter is?" The bewildered girl then broke down crying great big tears.

Wendy, unmoved in her reverie, began to speak. "Last night, I dreamt of a young man who was trying to save babies from being lost. Baby after baby kept falling out of his pram while his nurse was looking away. The young man could not save them all. The more babies were lost, the younger the man became until he was just a babe himself...lost like all the others."

Maimie thought for a moment while wiping her nose with the back of her hand. "Wendy, the babes in your dream, were none of them girls?" she asked in earnest.

"Oh no," Wendy answered gravely. "Girls, you know, are far too clever to fall out of their prams."

4

The Girl in the Theatre

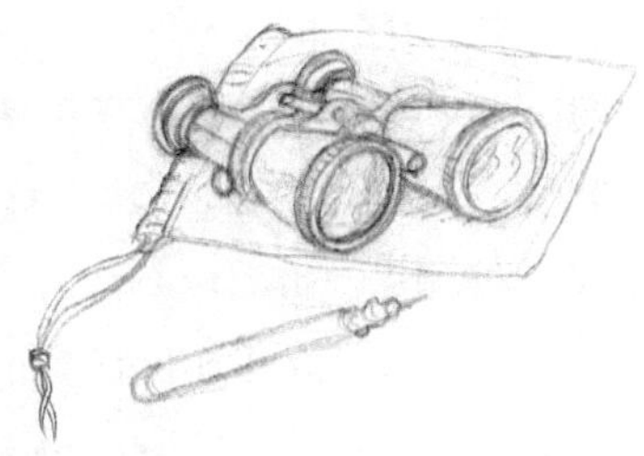

It seemed to Wendy that there were no words to describe the complexity of her life. How did one explain an existence overcome with inertia and, at the same time, hurtling forward toward the inevitable with momentum as unstoppable as a runaway train? On all sides, external forces were pressuring her to make a choice about something in which she had no choice.

So often, she had heard her elders speaking enviously about her youth and the promise of a wonderful future yet to come. Despite their words, she did not feel like she had her whole future ahead of her. On the contrary, Wendy felt that her life was on the verge of ending. She could clearly picture each phase as if she had already lived it. In the blink of an eye she would be a colorless, old woman—the end product of a predictable and safe life. Wendy knew with heartfelt certainty that the person she was, whom she was just beginning to understand, would start to disappear as soon as she became a wife.

Just last week, Maimie had reluctantly announced her engagement to an aging Viscount. It was a sensible match, giving the Sharpe family a title and replenishing the Viscount's dwindling wealth. When pressed, Wendy had said to her dearest friend that Viscount Withington of Perrin Hall was agreeable, but secretly, she was of the opinion that the aging count seemed more interested in his brandy and hunting dogs than his young bride-to-be. In truth, he was the type of husband that made a strong argument for the necessity of a lover.

Wendy sat up in bed, pushing her bed tray aside. Poor Maimie—to wed such an insipid man! Yet, the whole world seemed to smile on the match as respectable and sensible. And proper.

Where was the fire of Romeo and Juliet? Surely, the England of Shakespeare had awe-inspiring passion. Where had that romance gone? When had Britain grown so tepid and gray? Try as she might, Wendy could not recall to mind one marriage she had personally observed that exemplified all-encompassing love. Was she, like Maimie, doomed to be an agreeable wife to a passionless husband?

Putting on her slippers and robe, Wendy sat at her dressing table. She was certain James was close to proposing. For nearly a year, she'd succeeded in putting him off. Artfully, she had extolled the virtues of young men who were establishing themselves in business before taking a bride. Often, she had praised James for being among them. So far, not wanting to drop in her esteem, James had simply nodded along. Lately, however, he took great pains to impress upon her his occupational accomplishments. Being of the same world, Wendy knew that James experienced the same pressures as she. Caught in the same web, it was just a matter of time until they both did exactly what was expected of them.

Wendy brushed her hair absently—at least she had the theatre. The

Duke of York's Theatre had been her saving grace. It was passion in a world of propriety; bursting color in the sepia landscape of her life. It was her sanity. The theatre was the only place where Wendy truly felt alive.

Since her most recent birthday, Wendy had been allowed to attend the Saturday matinee performance with Maimie, unchaperoned. Yet the theatre, like everything in her life, had come at a price. It was no secret that Wendy's family was at the mercy of her Aunt's purse strings. Even her ability to go to the weekly matinee relied on the spinster's generosity and good will. In return, all Wendy needed to do was to *receive* James.

At the start, it had seemed like a small price to pay...to live.

Poor Wendy could not see that the true danger in compromise lies not in the act, itself, but in the precedent. Had she known the extent of her indebtedness and the price her heart would eventually pay, she would not have settled on the bargain so easily.

Every Saturday, Wendy Darling and Mamie Sharpe sat in the first row of the Royal Circle at the Duke of York's Theatre. No matter what the production, they assembled for their weekly dose of passion-infused freedom. As a result, the faithful friends would often see the same production more than once.

Wendy delighted in being able to discern the slightest difference in movement or lines. On their way home, she would share her observations with Maimie. "Irene outdid herself with the speech in act two today" or "Gerald seemed a bit off this afternoon, don't you think?" or "Nina was positively radiant!" Wendy regarded each performance with novelty regardless of how many times she had seen it. For Maimie, who was of an easily distracted nature, the novelty lay in being unchaperoned for the entire afternoon.

"What thrills you so about the theatre?" Maimie had once asked her friend as they were strolling through Kensington Gardens after their Sat-

urday matinee.

Wendy hardly knew where to begin. "The stories, the action, the sword-play–all of it! Oh Maimie, I wish I could have such adventures!'

"Wendy, such adventures are just stories. They do not exist in real life."

"But, dear Maimie, those same stories are created in the imaginations of playwrights, who are real people. Actors, who are real people, act them. One cannot write nor act what one does not know. So those stories must be based in some truth."

"Imagination is not truth, Wendy; it is the opposite of truth. It is escapism from the ordinary and dullness of our lives."

"Can a blind man understand what blue is? Or red?" countered Wendy vehemently. "That which springs forth from our imagination must have existed at some time in the past. Even if not evident here and now, our instinct tells us what we create is true. Imagination is where truth and instinct meet to form a world that has been, could be, and perhaps shall be again in the future. When you are watching a play can you not feel it?"

"No," replied her friend smiling devilishly. "Sometimes I feel sleepy, sometimes I feel hungry, and sometimes, if the actor is handsome, I feel...well, I shall just let you imagine the rest!"

Blushing at the memory, Wendy regarded herself in the mirror. She noticed a small scratch on her left cheek. The crimson welt had the appearance of a new wound. Thoughtfully, she ran her finger over it. Strange, she could not recall where it had come from. Perhaps she had scratched herself in the night. Looking over at her bed—disheveled as if she had been thrashing about—she frowned. Her sleep seemed to be growing more and more agitated.

Wendy gazed out the window, trying to recall the dream that had elicited such nocturnal movement. Had she been in a play? She remembered vivid colors more akin to stage scenery than real life. She had been on a great billowy cloud, staring down at a beautiful, mysterious island. Then she was falling...but not from the cloud. No, she was falling from something dark and sinister. Skull and crossbones flashed through her mind.

A pirate ship!

Like Mabel in Pirates of Penzance, she'd been captured by villainous pirates. They had forced her to walk the plank. She remembered standing on the coarse wood in her nightdress, shivering as a cold, stormy wind tugged cruelly at her hair. The plank began to retract forcing her to edge backwards toward the dark, tumultuous sea...a final step—then nothing. She was falling to her death. As she fell, her left cheek grazed the edge of the plank. Then—blackness.

Try as she might, she could not recall the rest of the dream. She felt sure, somehow, that there had been no splash. Wendy looked closer at the fresh scratch on her cheek. *What did it mean?*

The downstairs clock struck the hour shaking her from her reverie. Today, she and Maimie were to see a new production of The Three Mus-keteers. It was already ten o'clock and Wendy had much to do before her friend's arrival. Daydreaming could wait; now was the time for action.

Clutching his abdomen, Peter sat up in bed drenched in sweat. As far back as he could remember—that is to say, ever since the morning of his arrival at Smythe and Sons—his nights were troubled with mysterious and disturbing dreams. He'd been flying through a stormy sky over a dark and churning sea. A dark, menacing ship bobbed in the distance. As he flew toward the ship, its cannon opened fire with a thunderous crack. The cannonball hit him squarely in the stomach and he lost his air. Then he plunged into blackness.

No matter how hard he tried, he could not remember the rest of the dream...but somehow he knew there had not been a splash. Gingerly, he touched his tender stomach. What did it mean?

Peter heard movement in the next room. Griffin was stirring. Today being Saturday, the brothers would soon be making their pilgrimage to Trafalgar Square for what Griffin called Peter's "weekly communion."

More than a year ago, the brothers had observed a group of men in high boots and swords, making their way through Kensington Gardens. Greatly intrigued, Peter had insisted they follow the men to their destination, wherever it may be. And so the boys followed the strangers down streets and alleys, toward the Thames, and right thru the stage entrance of the Duke of York's Theatre. The men, as it turned out, were actors in the company and scheduled to rehearse the swordfight from *Romeo and Juliet*. Instantly, Peter was hooked!

For Peter, the theatre opened up a world of adventure that had previously existed only in his imagination. Before his eyes, the creations of Shakespeare, Wilde, Chekhov, Ibsen, and Shaw came to life full of wit and passion. Peter worshipped these actors; these men and women who could make him laugh or cry at their whim. Their characters touched his soul. Whether Shylock, Earnest, Treplev, or John Tanner; they spoke to him in truths, and he was richer for knowing them.

At first, the stage manager shooed the boys away, but at Peter's insistence, they returned week after week. However, since the theatre always had need of free labor, and since the crew quickly tired of tripping over them, they were promptly put to work backstage. For Peter, there was nothing better than being a part of the theatre. It became his first great love. Over the past year, he had done nearly every task from painting scenery to pulling the curtain. Ironically, it was in executing the latter task that Peter's great love was displaced by one even greater.

On the eve of Peter's birthday—or more accurately his anniversary of waking up on Sir William Smythe's doorstep—the assistant stage manager, known simply as Poole, let Peter pull the curtain for the matinee as a present. On Poole's command, Peter, in position in the left wing of the stage, began to pull the rope to open the curtain. As the veil between the stage and the audience parted, Peter had a clear view of the patrons in the first row of the Royal Circle.

It was her expression that instantly caught his attention. The look of expectancy and pure rapture on her face would have put the angels to shame! The play began, and she smiled releasing such undisguised joy that Peter, too, grinned from ear to ear.

She was the loveliest creature that Peter had ever seen. Not fashionably pale like so many young ladies her age, this girl seemed to glow with ruddy color. Her cheeks naturally blushed a rosy pink. Her full, rose-petal mouth conveyed volumes with even the slightest movement; a small smirk registered amusement; the tiniest pout hinted concern. Whether smiling in pleasure or biting her lower lip in distress, the effect was overwhelming.

She had large, perceptive blue eyes that overflowed with emotion and captured his being. When some action on stage caused her to look his way, she would stare down with eyes so bright that they seemed to bore two holes to the earth, and Peter lost sense of everything but her. Laughing or crying, the girl regarded the stage with such fierce passion that it caused Peter's heart to rise to his mouth.

Every Saturday, Peter stood transfixed in the stage shadows mastering the expressions of her beautiful face. It was apt—as Peter had learned through inquiry—that her name was Wendy Darling because nothing would ever be more darling to him than she.

Even now, alone in his room, the mere thought of her caused his heart to heave. Sighing, he closed his eyes wondering what her hair would smell like, whether she would feel hot or cold to his touch, what her voice would sound like murmuring softly against his chest?

Griffin, having never seen his brother so overcome or so helpless, had taken it upon himself to make inquiries as to the young lady's circumstances. Being the practical older brother, he tried to make Peter face reality of their different stations. But no matter what he argued, he could not sway Peter from the object of his affections.

"Peter," he reasoned. "She is your senior."

"True love cares nothing of age, Griffin."

"Wendy Darling is of good family. She will be a gentleman's wife."

"Don't you think that is for her to decide?"

"Peter, you know girls do not make such decisions; their families choose for them. Besides, she does not even know you exist!"

"She may not know of me yet, Griffin, but she can feel me." Peter smiled his most dazzling and cocky smile. "Relax, dear brother, I have a plan."

"What plan? You can barely function in her presence!"

"Griffin, what does my Wendy love above all else?"

"How should I know? I—we—you barely know her!"

"She loves theatre above all else."

"So?"

"So—I shall just have to become a part of what she loves best."

"Peter," exclaimed his brother. "You already have accomplished every job possible at the theatre, and she remains completely ignorant of your existence. What else is to be done?"

"Every job, save one," Peter replied. "Griffin, I mean to become an actor!"

Since his discovery of Wendy, Peter had waited patiently for an opportunity to take center stage at the theatre and in his beloved's heart. Little did he suspect, as he and Griffin hurried through the early morning streets to the Duke of York's Theatre, that fate was about to give him his chance.

5

D'Artagnon Takes Center Stage

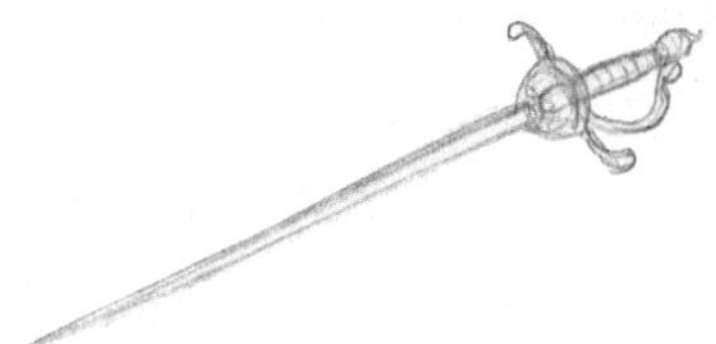

For those unfamiliar with the nature of the stage, the theatre is always a mass of energy prior to performances, and on the morning of a new production, its frantic pace seems to accelerate to a maddening speed. The Duke of York's Theatre was no exception. Therefore, Peter and Griffin were greatly surprised to be greeted backstage with frustrated inactivity. From the condition of the stage, sets and costumes asunder, it seemed that preparations had come to a screeching halt. Rather than making ready, cast and crew gathered in tight knots as if awaiting inspiration or guidance.

"Poole," Griffin inquired in a hushed tone. "Why is everyone standing about? Has something happened?"

"Oh tragedy! Ruin!" replied the assistant, with all the dramatic emphasis befitting his occupation. "The play cannot open! It is a sad day for the Duke of York's Theatre." As if to emphasize the point, Poole blew his nose loudly.

"But what prevents *The Three Musketeers* from opening today? Yesterday everything seemed in perfect readiness."

"It is our D'Artagnon. Granville injured his arm practicing the great swordfight in Act Five. See, he cannot even hold his weapon! We cannot present *The Three Musketeers* without a D'Artagnon!"

The boys looked at Granville, who made a stoic, although unsuccessful, effort to raise his sword. The director, Dion Boucicault (pronounced Boo-see-kO), thundered about, pausing now and then to scowl at the injured actor. "What good is it if you can hold the thing? If you cannot wield D'Artagnon's sword, then we shall be forced to cut all the great fight scenes! Why don't we cut off the Musketeers' testicles while we are at it?! No, the play will not go on!"

Peter stepped forward, speaking for the first time, "Mr. Boucicault, I can do it."

"What?" He looked Peter up and down skeptically. "Aren't you one half of the pair of little stage mice that are always lurking about? No, I'm afraid we will have to cancel."

"Give me a chance, Sir. I can do it. I know every word by heart!"

"It is not merely a matter of words, boy. It is a matter of passion, and feeling—and—and fencing."

Poole cut in. "The boy can fence."

"It is not just a matter of fencing," the director continued. "It is a matter of feeling and passion and—"

As Mr. Boucicault delivered his speech, Peter walked over to Granville and asked for his sword. Brandishing the sword, he turned to the Fight Captain, Monsieur Girrold.

"Engarde!"

Monsieur Girrold drew his sword in answer and a wonderful freeform swordfight began. At first, the captain was easy on the boy, but as Peter exhibited his apparent skill, the man began to respond without reluctance. As M. Girrold thrust, Peter parried each move without hesitation. Soon the boy gained the advantage relegating his opponent to a somewhat frantic defense. Like a whirling dervish possessed, Peter cut, parried, and twirled across the stage in a most impressive display. Only when he had bested the Fight Captain, separating him from his weapon, did he look at Mr. Boucicault, who in turn was staring at Monsieur Girrold. The entire company, who had been watching, broke out in enthusiastic applause.

"The boy is D'Artagnon incarnate!" exclaimed the breathless Captain as he retrieved his sword. "Peter, surely you were a swashbuckler in another life! Where did you learn to do that?"

Peter shrugged.

"He has always been able to do that," Griffin replied proudly.

Shaking his head, Mr. Boucicault bellowed to the company, "What are you waiting for? Get the boy in costume, practice the fight sequences, and run the lines to all D'Artagnon's scenes. After all, the show must go on!"

His dream finally within his grasp, Peter rushed to get ready, so overjoyed he thought he might crow.

Wendy seated herself excitedly in the first row of the Royal Circle and began examining her programme. She loved the story of the Three Musketeers and greatly anticipated this new production. Over the past fortnight, she had worked herself into more than one agitation trying to visualize the cast enacting her most beloved scenes. Little did she realize how much the production would exceed her expectations.

The girl scanned the curtained stage. Something more than anticipation tugged at her hopes. A pull, nearly magnetic in nature, caused her eyes to fix on the far right corner—the actors' stage left—as if the meaning of life, itself, were there and about to reveal all its mysteries to her.

"Wendy dear," exclaimed Maimie pulling out a handsomely feathered fan. "The play has not yet begun and already you are flushed and trembling. You must try to calm yourself. You will never attract a husband in such a tizzy."

At the word *husband* Wendy looked up sharply. "Do not even presume to joke about such matters, Maimie. James will not be put off much longer. Father and Mother seem to quarrel fortnightly about how to press him for an engagement. Aunt Mildred shamelessly flatters his great aunt and grandmamma. Even the dressmaker is dropping hints. Every time she comes, she brings sketches of the latest wedding gown designs from Paris. I am at my wit's end! Truly you and this theatre are the only bits of peace afforded me."

"Even this," Maimie gestured around her, "may soon be coming to an end. Mother says that once I marry, it will not do for the Viscountess Withington of Perrin Hall to appear in society unchaperoned and without her husband. Guessing on Lord Withington's tastes, I shall be doomed to a box at the Opera."

"The Opera?" Wendy exclaimed in horror and grasped her friend's hand. "Oh Maimie, what will I do when you become a bride? I shall die of loneliness."

"You will marry, too, and everything will turn out right in the end. You will see."

Shaking her head, Wendy closed her eyes and sighed. "Aunt Mildred is odious indeed, but for the sake of this," indicating the theatre with a sweep of her hand, "I shall have to endure."

"If only you married, you would gain independence from the old spinster's iron fist."

"And trade it for the control of a husband? I have always wanted a family of my own, to be a mother, but at what cost, dear friend?"

An expectant hush fell over the theatre. Wendy turned her attention again toward the stage to see Mr. Charles Frohman, the producer and an American, standing before them.

"Ladies and Gentlemen, the part of D'Artagnon will be played by Peter...uh...Peter...um...Neverland—Peter Neverland, who will be making his stage debut."

Wendy's eyebrows raised in surprise. *Peter Neverland?* She'd never heard of him. A quick glance at Maimie confirmed he was unknown to her as well.

The curtain rose while Wendy leaned perilously forward, scanning the stage in annoyance. D'Artagnon was one of her favorite literary characters. She had been looking forward to Granville's portrayal. The role would require skill and subtlety—no novice to the stage could do it justice. *And besides...that is...and...*

Wendy's train of thought abruptly derailed, for D'Artagnon had stepped from the very spot where her eyes had previously alighted. As he took center stage, everything else ceased to exist. For her, the world had become pitch black except for one shining spotlight causing the young man below to glow as if lit by the sun itself. He was not merely an actor but an angel—D'Artagnon incarnate!

To say the actor was handsome was an understatement. He had not the delicate features of some pretty men. No. For lack of a better description, he was breathtaking!

His thick chestnut hair had a slight curl with copper and golden highlights that shimmered under the stage lights. He had a straight, aristocratic nose and his square chin bore a delectable cleft. When he smiled, his generous mouth revealed white, straight teeth and deeply dimpled cheeks.

His dazzling eyes were by far his most striking attribute. Deep emerald green, colored with flecks of gold and mahogany, they were terrible and sublime all at once. They seemed to search Wendy out in the darkness. Caught in their gaze, she felt transparent as he stared up at her with eyes so bright that they seemed to bore two holes to the Heavens.

Although he was the height and size of a man, he had a discernable boyishness to him. It was the kind of combination, Wendy reflected, that made him appear older than his actual years but would, in later life, make him seem considerably younger. Coupled with his unrestrained zeal, his appearance made him glorious—god-like. Wendy could not take her eyes off him.

For the next three hours, there was only Peter. The play, the actors, the words meant nothing to her. Every time he exited the stage, Wendy bit her lower lip in anguish. Without realizing she was doing so, she held her breath as long as she dared. Staring at the wing, she willed him to return so she could breathe again.

The final act contained a thrilling swordfight. Peter was magnificent! He was so sure and brave that Wendy felt certain he was a swashbuckler in a previous life.

As the curtain closed, the audience rose to its feet, as one, but Wendy could not move. Overcome with emotion, her whole body trembled with an unexpected force. She ached with the need to know Peter; longed to bare her soul to him—confide her every thought and fear—without restraint. She needed to consume every scrap of information Peter could give her and this need felt very close to madness.

If she had been capable of rational thought, she would've had an epiphany as to why so many of Shakespeare's plays ended in tragedy. For the line that separates true love from insanity thinned to the point of transparency. But Wendy had no such insight.

The unfortunate girl was undone.

Eyes closed and shivering, she sat for the longest time in torment. Finally, with Maimie's pleading and the insistence of the head of ushers, Wendy left the darkened theatre feeling more confused and alone than she had in her whole life. It seemed her entire existence began and ended in that single afternoon alongside the story of D'Artagnon...and the actor, Peter Neverland.

It would seem improbable, impossible even, that two people who'd never spoken could form such an immediate and earth-shattering attachment at first sight. Very few have the aptitude to see it and even fewer the propensity to experience it. But you should understand, there are unseen forces at work.

If one were to look toward the Neverlands, a certain island would appear to be waking up. Through the mist, we can just glimpse the first stirrings of spring after an interminable, frozen winter. Furthermore, Wendy and Peter are not unknown to one another, even if both have forgotten and remain quite ignorant of their previous acquaintance. Despite thinking themselves strangers, each felt as if they had danced a hundred dances and shared a summer's worth of conversation with the other.

And now that we understand the way of it, let us draw closer to discover what each makes of this most fortuitous encounter.

At Peter's urging, Griffin took up a permanent station in the stage left wing. From that position he could observe Wendy and report to Peter between scenes.

It was from that vantage Peter had been waiting with his brother just prior to curtain, when Mr. Frohman made his announcement. "Ladies and Gentlemen, the part of D'Artagnon will be played by Peter...uh...Peter...um..." Having forgotten Peter's surname, he glanced helplessly toward the brothers.

But before Griffin could say Smythe, Peter blurted out, "Neverland."

Flustered, Frohman continued, "Neverland—Peter Neverland, who will be making his stage debut."

Griffin raised his dark eyebrows whispering, "Neverland?"

"A stage name, Brother. In case of disaster, I would hate for this to reflect on Father." At the moment of decision, it had popped into his mind, unbidden. And although he could not articulate his reasons, he rather liked the name. It felt exotic and comfortable at the same time, like a well-loved treasure from abroad.

As the curtain rose, Peter looked to Wendy in the audience. Putting his hand on his heart, he sighed heavily. "Look how she leans forward in anticipation."

Actors began taking the stage while Peter listened anxiously for his cue. His hand slipped automatically into his right pocket, searching for his good luck charm. Superstitiously, he lifted it to his mouth and kissed it. *Oh love, do not fail me nor forsake me.* His cue. Tucking the talisman safely away, he took up his destiny center stage.

Three hours later, he returned to the same spot to consult Griffin. He'd been so greatly heartened by his brother's reports between scenes that during the curtain call he had openly held Wendy's celestial gaze.

His bows had been for her alone.

Although responsive throughout the play, his Wendy now seemed distraught. She did not stand with the house, in fact she hardly moved. Instead, she examined him with such intensity that Peter felt she was trying to see into his very soul.

Even after the curtain closed, Peter continued to watch Wendy from the shadows trying to guess the meaning of her reserved, unexpected reaction. "Why does she not move? She did seem to enjoy the play, did she not, Griffin?"

"Aye, Peter, she did."

"And did she not laugh, smile, cry, and cheer in earnest?"

"In truth, as I have told you, she did all those things."

"Then why does she yet sit there so pale? Oh Griffin, perhaps she is ill."

"Peter!" Mr. Boucicault's booming voice resounded from backstage. "Peter! Where are you? Everyone is waiting to congratulate you!"

Peter bit his cheek in agitation. "Griffin, will you please go tell everyone that I will be there presently?"

"Aye, Peter."

In the stillness, Peter watched, astounded, as a subdued Wendy was led away by her companion and the head of ushers. Her departure left him feeling unsettled and vaguely bereft, as if his life had been placed on pause.

Completely alone, he slipped his good luck charm out of his right pocket and lifted it to his lips. When he awoke on the doorstep of Smythe and Sons, it was the sole possession on his person, and he was never without it. Like him, it was a mystery. To Peter, the talisman was what he wished on—where he stored his hopes and dreams—but to others it was just a little broken half of a porcelain thimble.

As had happened many times before, Peter's dream guide came to him in his sleep. She was a tiny, beautiful winged creature illuminated from within and the size of his fist. Though she spoke to Peter in musical tones that had no speech, Peter understood her all the same. "Take me to Wendy," he commanded and the bright spirit took off in flight with Peter following close behind. They sailed over London and into the night sky. To Peter, it seemed like years that they flew, over oceans and strange lands, following stars. Finally, they approached a lone island rising from the sea. That wild, primitive land seemed a strange place to encounter Wendy.

As the guide led him across a sparkling lagoon and into the dense jungle, her pace quickened. Dodging branches and giant leaves, Peter struggled to keep up. The spirit was getting too far ahead, and he could barely make out her glow in the distance.

"Please slow down!" he shouted in vain.

As she vanished from view, it occurred to him that the guide had purposely taken him to this place to lose him, and that his dear Wendy was still back in London asleep in her bed. The spiteful creature had led Peter to the opposite end of the earth and meant for him to never return...

That night was the first time Wendy dreamt of the little pixie. Wendy stood alone on the darkened stage when an illuminating glow appeared before her. She was exceedingly happy to be rescued from darkness and by such an exotic and lovely creature. Although she did not understand what the beautiful creature was saying, she did understand that the pixie was offering to take her to Peter.

Without hesitation, she followed as her glowing guide led her down into the bowels of the theatre. They seemed to go for hours through an unending labyrinth of damp corridors and dusty staircases. The further down they went, the faster the pixie seemed to go. Running, Wendy barely made it to each corner in time to seem where the glowing guide turned next.

"Please wait!" she begged.

Stumbling, she was again in darkness. It then occurred to her that the delicate creature had intended for this all along. Peter was probably on the stage this very moment looking for her. Lost and alone, Wendy knew beyond certainty she was never meant to make it back...

6

A Knock at the Door

*N*othing horrid was visible in the air, yet Peter's progress had become slow and labored, exactly as if he were pushing his way through hostile forces. Sometimes he hung in the air until he had to beat on it with his fist.

They don't want me to land, *Peter thought. But he could not say who "they" were. With great effort, he touched down in a glade. At his feet, laid Wendy, a mass of blonde curls in a nightdress and as still as the grave.*

"She is dead," he said uncomfortably. "Perhaps she is frightened at being dead."

He started to turn away, but Wendy's arm stayed him (for, indeed, she was not dead but merely very ill and in peril of dying). "If she lies here," Peter bemoaned, "she will die."

Then Peter had a wonderful idea. He would build a little house round her that would protect her until she recovered. Kneeling, Peter declared to Wendy, "I am your servant. If only you could tell me which type of house you like best?"

Wendy stirred in her sleep. Her lovely mouth opened into a perfect 'O' and without opening her eyes, she began to sing:

"I wish I had a pretty house,

Gay windows all about.

With roses peeping in, you know,

And babies peeping out."

A tiny house with red walls and a mossy green roof appeared around her. The house was quite beautiful, and no doubt Wendy was very cozy within, though, of course, Peter could no longer see her. He desired more than anything to go inside and watch over Wendy, but as he approached the door, he realized there was no knocker. "However am I to enter," Peter lamented, "if I cannot knock?"

He scoured the glade until he found the discarded heel of a shoe, which had the makings of an excellent knocker. Triumphant, he turned back to the little house only to find it gone—and Wendy with it. Both had been carried off by the elusive "they." Blinking at the empty glade before him, Peter wondered if he would ever see his Wendy again.

For nearly a week, Peter could not shake the image of an ailing Wendy being led from the theatre. Worry that she was unwell gripped his heart, casting a pall over the joy that should have been his successful theatre debut. He needed to know she was in good health before his grip on sanity became lost to all-consuming fear.

The Thursday before the following Saturday matinee, Mr. Frohman announced his intention to throw a grand ball for theatre patrons. The event, to be held in a month's time, would serve dual purposes: an endeavor to increase private donations and an opportunity to celebrate the successful run of *The Three Musketeers* with the triumphant debut of their very own stage mouse, Peter. For Peter, the news meant an even greater purpose, the very excuse needed to ascertain Wendy Darling's state of being.

Pacing back and forth in the front office of Smythe and Sons Accounting Firm the next morning, Peter anxiously awaited the arrival of his elder brother. When Griffin entered, he had scarcely had a moment to remove his muffler and greatcoat before being set upon.

"Peter," Griffin reprimanded. For he knew the source of his younger brother's worry as well as he knew himself. "You must calm yourself. On the morrow you can assure yourself that Miss Darling is well."

Peter smiled, a fierce gleam sparked in his jewel-like eyes. "I shan't have to endure the agony of another day. If you are willing to help me—" Anxiety replaced his grin as he pleaded, "You will help me, won't you, Griffin?"

"Aye." Griffin was well enough acquainted with Peter's schemes to trust it would be equal parts benign intent and ill-conceived impulsiveness. However, where his brother's mental peace was concerned, Griffin would endeavor to aid in his peace of mind.

"Thank you," Peter replied and produced a sealed invitation address to Wendy in elegant script. "This is an invitation to Mr. Frohman's grand ball. Will you deliver it to Miss Darling?"

"Aye, Peter."

As Griffin began to shrug back into his coat, Peter added, "And wait for a reply by her own and most dear hand?"

"Aye." Griffin began to rewind his muffler round his neck until Peter snatched the end and halted his progress.

"And—confirm she is in good health?"

Although this seemed like a lot to ask of a mere messenger, Griffin merely nodded and extended his hand for the invitation.

As Peter handed over the parchment, he acknowledged with a small measure of chagrin, "For the life of me, I cannot fathom why you indulge me so."

Although meant as rhetorical, Griffin took the question to heart. With a far-away look in his ebony eyes, he answered, "In truth, it's because I feel as though you took me in, rather than the other way around. I cannot explain it, but sometimes in the twilight of waking, I dream that I'm scared and lost and you rescue me." He shook his head to dispel the vision. "Just a fancy, I suppose. Be assured I will execute your errand to the exact detail."

Watching his brother's retreating form, Peter marveled at his fortune. Providence had quite easily brought him a family and love at first sight. Although unable to recall life before Highbury Street, he felt sure that he must've done something noble to earn such a goodly lot. Griffin's frank words, while improbable, only lent credence to this idea.

Now we know how Peter rescued forgotten babes and guided those lost boys until they were on the verge of manhood. Each and every boy deposited back into Kensington Gardens had the highest moral character. They entered adolescence fearlessly and grew up to become brave men who made their mark on our world. Some of the most influential men in our history were produced in just such a way. But those are stories for another time.

I hope you want to know what became of Wendy and whether she recovered from her first encounter with Peter Neverland. By the time she arrived home from the Duke of York's matinee, she was quite herself again. At least on the outside... Her insides were a jumble of thoughts and emotions surfacing for the first time.

On the morning of this particular part of our story, she was in the drawing-room, taking her regular instruction from Aunt Mildred. Later in the day, the women of the Darling household, along with Aunt Mildred, were expected at the Whitby's for tea. Mrs. Darling sat silently by, her sentiments belied only by the twitching of the perfectly conspicuous kiss in the right had corner of her sweet, mocking mouth. Wendy, you should know, had inherited that very same mouth and kiss.

"This is a test," Aunt Mildred admonished shrilly. "The Whitby's want to ensure your moral caliber and refinement is up to snuff. Come Wendy! Let us practice for this afternoon's event." She then began to advise Wendy on the genteel art of making conversation without saying anything at all. Wendy, however, kept getting distracted by the old woman's waddle, which bobbed and wiggled above the ruffle of the woman's high collar.

When a knock on the door interrupted the discourse, both Wendy, who'd been fixating on her great aunt's throat rather than her discourse, and Mrs. Darling, who retained yet enough girlishness to balk at the matriarch's practical lessons, were secretly thankful for the interruption.

A moment later, Old Liza appeared with a pretty little invitation. "For Wendy, Ma'am." The servant offered the parchment not to Wendy but to Great Aunt Mildred. You see, the servant had been in the Darling household since she was a slight girl, and she knew on which side of the family their income's bread was buttered. If not for Great Aunt Mildred, she would've been discharged a long time ago. For the Darling's third child squeaked by so narrowly, Liza felt sure without the good matriarch's intervention she would've been put out on the street so that he could afford to stay.

"What is this?" Great Aunt Mildred's face turned fish-like, all pursed lips and narrowness as she inspected the invitation. "It seems," she said to Wendy at last. "The producer of that theater you love so is throwing a ball."

"A ball!"

It was Mrs. Darling who spoke thus, fortunately taking the attention off Wendy and the tremor that instantly racked her body at the thought of dancing with a certain young actor. Mrs. Darling's liking for parties was one of her most remarkable qualities. Turning to her only daughter, she clapped her hands in delight, exclaiming, "Oh, I shall have occasion to lend you the necklace that George gave me! It does go so perfectly with your bracelet."

Wendy loved to lend her pearl and ruby bracelet to her mother. It did complement Mrs. Darling's necklace as if they were a matched set; therefore, on many occasions Mrs. Darling had asked for the loan of it. Imagining Peter's reaction to how fine she would look adorned in them gave Wendy a small thrill.

"May I go, Aunt Mildred?" Wendy asked, trying to make the monumental inquiry seem trivial.

"Please, dear Aunt Mildred," Mrs. Darling echoed. "Mayn't she go?"

During this discourse, Old Liza had been quite forgotten until she cleared her throat and with downcast eyes said, "I'm to give the messenger Wendy's reply, Ma'am."

"Of course." Aunt Mildred crossed to the writing desk, penned a short reply and handed it to the maid. By way of dismissal, she ordered, "Give him this."

Liza left with a scowl, for she did not like the look of this particular messenger at all and was eager to be rid of him. Besides being too well dressed, he possessed the dark hair and eyes of a Spaniard. He also kept inquiring into Miss Darling's health, an inappropriate and annoying impertinence in the old servant's humble opinion.

Neither of the Darling women were given the benefit of seeing Great Aunt Mildred's reply. For a tense moment, mother and daughter agonized over Wendy's fate, for the girl's attendance relied not only on the old woman's agreement but also in her generosity to finance a suitable gown for the event.

After a pause befitting the Matriarch's stature and influence over the situation, Great Aunt Mildred magnanimously declared, "I suppose, it never hurts for a young lady, who has yet to make her social mark, to partake in respectable society."

At this, Wendy and Mrs. Darling clasped hands and began to dance about the room in a happy romp. It reminded Wendy of the lovely dances they used to have in the old nursery when she was still a child. Back then, Mrs. Darling would pirouette so wildly that all you could see of her was her kiss, and then if you had dashed at her, you might have gotten it.

"Mother," Wendy asked when they finally stopped to catch their breath. "How did you know you were in love with father?"

The enigmatic kiss in the corner of Mrs. Darling's smile grew deeper. "Why it was love at first sight, dear."

This was an apt statement. As a girl, Mrs. Darling has been bursting with romantic sensibilities. When she finally decided she was ready to fall in love, Mr. Darling had the distinction of being the very first to arrive on her doorstep.

The way Mr. Darling won her was this: the many gentlemen who had been boys when she was a girl discovered simultaneously that they loved her, and they all ran to her house to propose to her except Mr. Darling, who took a cab and nipped in first, and so he got her. This confirmed Mr. Darling's notion that love at first sight sometimes had more to do with positioning than providence.

"How wonderful," Wendy sighed, Great Aunt Mildred and her odious lessons momentarily forgotten. "Love at first sight."

As Wendy floated from the room, Great Aunt Mildred's eyes narrowed in shrewd speculation. Until that moment, she had not the least bit of concern in letting her great niece attend Mr. Frohman's ball. Suddenly, the occasion seemed rife with peril. If the girl had ulterior motives... Still, she had given her word that Wendy could attend and she would stand by her promise. However, that didn't mean that certain precautions couldn't be taken.

Great Aunt Mildred had ulterior motives of her own, you see. Those motives, when coupled with manipulation, could make even the most well-meaning matriarch a formidable adversary. And the art of manipulation was, after all, a skill that the old woman had perfected in spades.

* * *

Unsure if she was awake or dreaming, Wendy watched as her night-light blinked and gave such a yawn that all the other night-lights in the house yawned also. Before they could close their mouths, they all went out. Although she wasn't afraid of the dark, she did not want them to go. For night-lights are the eyes a mother leaves behind to guard her children.

There was another light in the room now, a thousand times brighter than the night-lights, but in the time we have taken to say this, Wendy, herself, issued a great yawn and nodded off. In the second before reaching oblivion, a shadow flitted across the light and began to sob.

7

The Way of Things

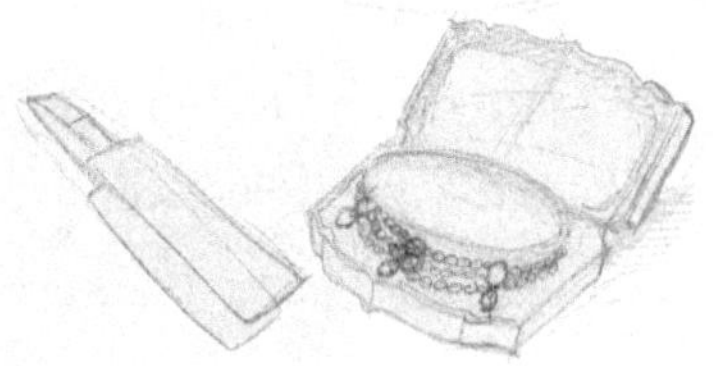

As is the way of things, fate often conspires to intervene where we, ourselves, are incapable of action. It was no different for Peter and Wendy. Unable to transcend their own faults, the Heavens had decided a ball would be just the thing to bring the two together. For no difference in stations or circumstances could thwart the will of Divine Providence.

Wendy admired herself appreciatively in her full-length mirror. The neckline of her new rose-colored gown dipped just low enough, the waist cinched just tight enough, and the tulle and satin beaded skirt just full enough that her form achieved a perfect hourglass. Her shiny, golden curls were fastened with pearl combs, a perfect complement to the ruby and pearl jewelry set. She colored her lips, pinched her cheeks, and then smiled in awe. For the first time in her life, she felt as beautiful as she looked—more than beautiful, she felt radiant. For the first time she could remember, Wendy felt *free*.

It was love.

She finally understood what Aunt Mildred and her elders spoke of so enviously. It had been a month since Peter Neverland triumphantly claimed the London stage; and with it, her heart. Love of Peter had opened up a completely new life for her, one brimming with exciting possibility. Without him, she would probably already be Mrs. James Christopher Whitby II. But Peter filled every day, tantalizing her imagination with the promise of tomorrow. Long pleasant hours were spent imagining the life they could have together as husband and wife.

We would be remiss not to point out that in these imaginings a tiny part of Wendy's makeup desired to mother Peter as well, but she squelched the feeling as childish. She had yet to admit to herself the want of mothering is an elemental part of the attraction every young woman feels for a young man and such urges should never be discarded as immature. Wendy, of all people, should have known that.

Unfortunately, preoccupation with love and the challenges of being grown left little room in her head for reflection. Under obligation to her patroness aunt, she constantly juggled thoughts of Peter and James. Just last Saturday Wendy had returned from the matinee to find James waiting for her in the garden. Still under the enchantment of Peter Neverland, James seemed even more lackluster, and the comparison served to strengthen her resolve. She listened as James calmly recounted his professional accomplishments to date and then just as dispassionately asked her to become his wife.

Her cool reply had been equally as impassive. *"James, I am flattered. But now, I cannot."*

She meant *I know* now *what can be possible in life. I know how it feels to love with one's entire being, and I cannot go back.* Now, *Peter has come into my life and no other will satisfy me.* James, she suspected, took her to mean that it was merely a matter of timing and perhaps there would be a chance sometime in the future, so he did not press her further. Her refusal was easier than she had ever dared hope.

While refusing James had been easy, explaining her actions to her elders took considerable more effort and skill. She knew that Aunt Mildred and her mother, who was under the old woman's influence, would certainly challenge her decision. Therefore, she sought the most formidable ally in the household, her father.

While the bearish Mr. Darling was thick skulled and socially inept, he did have quite a gentle spot for his only daughter. Since all fathers are reluctant to be replaced in their daughter's lives by husbands, Wendy appealed to his fatherly vanity.

As Mr. Darling sat at his desk engaged in calculations, Wendy decided to soften him up by asking about his favorite subject. With a coy smile, that she hoped conveyed the proper balance of interest and ignorance, she inquired, "How is business, Father?"

Pausing in his work, he indulged Wendy with a patriarchal smile. He didn't expect Wendy, or any female for that matter, to grasp the complexities of business but he did rather enjoy being an authority on the subject. "Stocks are up and shares are down," he said. He was one of those deep ones who know an awfully lot about stocks and shares. Of course, no one really knows, but he quite seemed to know, and all the women in the Darling household respected him for this. Even odious Aunt Mildred.

With a small sigh, Wendy replied, "I suppose soon, I shall have to rely on James for such important information."

While one hundred percent in favor of Wendy making a favorable match, and as much as he approved of her intended's profession as a banker, Mr. Darling did not particularly like the idea of someone else becoming the expert in his daughter's life. The thought of her looking at some other man with all respect and admiration she currently held for him caused a sharp sensation, much like heartburn, to seize his chest.

"James is an intelligent lad," he extolled. "But he lacks the experience only decades of hard work can provide."

"You are so wise, Father." Again, Wendy sighed, this time with more force of emotion behind the gesture. "If only I didn't have to leave you so soon. If only I had a little more time."

There is a soft, secret place in a father's heart that can only be touched by the wishes of a daughter. Wendy's entreaties burrowed into that spot and took root. Until now, Mr. Darling had viewed the matter of Wendy's engagement as a societal concern. You see, he had a passion for being exactly like his neighbours, and since all of their daughters had married young and well, he could allow nothing less for Wendy. He had his position in the city to consider.

Fortunately, the spot in his heart that only Wendy could influence overshadowed external concerns, making it easy to acquiesce. Such fondness Mr. Darling felt for her as he patted her hand and offered, "You need not leave until you are ready, child. You are barely a woman and hardly a spinster. If you require more time with your family, you may have it."

"Thank you." Wendy kissed her father sweetly on the cheek. Having nearly everything she wanted from him, she let agitation chase the smile from her face for her final request. "Oh dear. How can I possibly tell Mother and dear Aunt Mildred? They will be so terribly disappointed with me. I cannot bear to be the cause of such upset. I don't suppose you might tell them for me?"

I am responsible for it all, thought Mr. Darling. *I, George Darling, have allowed my only daughter to be pushed into marriage and banished from her home. Mea culpa, mea culpa.* You see, he had had a classical education, and embraced every opportunity to ensure it did not go to waste. Even the unpleasant ones. Ever predictable, Mr. Darling told his daughter to take all the time she needed and not to worry; he would speak to the ladies.

How Wendy loved him for his faults!

Since neither her mother nor outspoken Aunt Mildred had said one word to her, she concluded that her father had been most persuasive. In fact, her female relations had been surprisingly compliant. When she asked for a new gown, her aunt summoned the dressmaker at her own expense, while her mother offered to help her with her hair.

Dressed in her finery, Wendy felt as if she had stepped through the looking glass. The tight ball of dread in the pit of her stomach at the prospect of her future vanished, making everything seem vibrant and new. Even the woman staring back at her in the mirror was a beautiful and very grown-up stranger.

Still under the spell of the mirror, she picked up the invitation from the bureau and ran her fingers over the raised elegant gold script.

You are cordially invited to the home of Mr. Charles Frohman for a grand ball to celebrate the success of The Three Musketeers.

The whole company would be there, including Peter! Her heart began to pound in anticipation as she carefully tucked the invitation into her handbag and held it to her breast.

Taking a step back toward the center of the room, Wendy dropped into a demure curtsey before practicing the Boston Waltz in long gliding steps. How would it feel to be in Peter's arms at last? Twirling across the floor, she imagined for the hundredth time the monumental conversation she would have with Peter later that evening. Perhaps the most important conversation of her life.

Mid-spin, Wendy halted. With a small frown, she stepped toward the foot of her window. Scattered around the floor were a curious assortment of leaves that has certainly not been there when she went to bed. You see, even from infancy Wendy had always been a tidy child, and the trait had merely increased with age.

Kneeling for closer examination revealed they were skeleton leaves, but she was sure they did not come from any tree that grew in England. She peered at the floor for marks of a strange foot and, finding none, stood to inspect the window itself. She looked through the weathered pane into the garden below. It was a sheer drop of thirty feet, without so much as a spout to climb up by. The trellis, of course, stood near, but it appeared unmolested.

Yet, something about the leaves seemed familiar. If only she could recall the previous night's dream. Reaching through the thick veil that separates the waking from dreams, she recollected sobbing. Something had come too near, trying to break through. An elusive shadow...

If you or I had been there, we should have seen the shadow was the Neverlands in the guise of a boy very like Wendy Darling's kiss. He was a lovely boy, clad in skeleton leaves and the juices that ooze out of trees; but the most entrancing thing about him was that he had all his first teeth. When he saw she was all but grown-up, he gnashed the little pearls at her.

Wendy, unfortunately, remembered naught about her dream visitor but the sob of his shadow. In the street below, a motorcar chugged up the lane and braked to a stop outside No. 14. Mysterious dreams and leaves forgotten, her heart skipped a beat and she took a moment to regain her equilibrium. With one final check in the mirror, a very grown-up Wendy descended to the waiting vehicle that would deliver her to her destiny.

If only she had not put away her childhood so neatly, she might have recognized the shadow. She might also have heard the quiet voice beseeching her from the nursery. For the voice of her inner child pleaded to come along. Had she taken young Wendy with her, she might have recognized the boy of the skeleton leaves on sight...and in doing so, discovered her true destiny.

For the hundredth time Peter straightened his black bowtie. He ran his fingers through his thick, unruly hair and practiced a dazzling smile into the upstairs hall mirror. The dashing gentleman in the tuxedo who smiled back at him possessed a self-assurance that bordered on cocky. And why should he not be considering the recent triumphs in his life?

Peter was living in a dream. Overnight, he had conquered the London stage. Invited into the best parlors, introduced to an endless array of wealthy, eligible daughters, he was suddenly the toast of high society. Welcomed and adored by all he met, he could do no wrong.

Tonight, Mr. Frohman had orchestrated this ball as much to celebrate the success of Peter as the play. Theatre patrons were clamoring for the company of Peter Neverland. He knew the fame was not really real, just another kind of play. Nevertheless, Peter found it intoxicating!

Complying with Mr. Frohman's wish for him to make a grand entrance, Peter waited restlessly in the upstairs hall of the producer's great house on Trafalgar Square. Below him, the main floor vibrated with activity and music. It seemed nearly all of London society had turned out to worship him. All that remained was the arrival of the one person that mattered most. Wendy Darling was his reason—*the* reason he was here—and he could scarcely believe she would soon be in his arms.

For a moment, Peter worried she had changed her mind and would not attend. But Peter's very nature was one of nearly fatal optimism. Personally, he had confirmed the delivery of Miss Darling's invitation and acceptance from her very own and very dear hand. She would come and before the night drew to a close, her heart would be his.

Since the ball's inception, Peter had occupied his every waking hour while not on stage with happy anticipation. This evening, he would finally know how it felt to hold her; to speak to her, at long last. How he had envisioned his declaration to Wendy—he knew every word by heart! She, of course, would melt to him, and her beautiful cerulean eyes would shine with reverence.

By habit, he slipped his hand into his pocket and, grasping his good luck charm, made a wish. *Make Wendy mine.* As if in answer, Griffin appeared at the foot of the stairs nodding and gesturing wildly. Miss Darling had arrived.

Descending the main staircase, Peter reflected on how Wendy had brought him to this place. Although he had discovered the theatre on his own, without her influence, would he have loved it as much? Would he have formed the resolve to forsake his father's business and become an actor? It was for love of Wendy that Peter was becoming the man he felt certain he was meant to be. And not just a man in the narrowest definition of a grown male, but as protector, provider, and—dare he be so bold?—sweetheart. So many times he had imagined this; their first meeting, professing his love, taking her for his bride and growing old together in love. Now that the moment was at hand, he could scarcely breathe!

Just last night he had dreamt of them as children, playing father and mother as if in rehearsal for future bliss.

He affectionately called her "old lady" when she met him at the door with their make-believe brood.

She went to him and put her hand on his shoulder. "Dear Peter," she said. "I'm afraid I have passed my best, but you don't want to exchange me, do you?"

"No Wendy." Certainly, he did not want a change. Whether young and brimming with possibility or mature and radiating experience, she

was perfection. His dream-self watched the boy Peter and the girl Wendy pretending. For a split second, he felt terribly old and wished, instead of Father, his role could be that of Wendy's devoted son.

Peter came to uncomfortably, blinking, you know, like one not sure whether he was awake or asleep. Had he actually felt afraid to become a husband to Wendy? To start a family and grow old with her? Such lapses in confidence, even when dreaming, were so foreign to Peter that he easily shook them off.

At the bottom of the stairs, Griffin waited. With unwavering approval, he adjusted his brother's pocket kerchief and straightened his tie.

"She's here?" Peter inquired, his devastating grin ready to wreak havoc.

"Aye, Peter." Griffin nodded toward the far end of the hall. "She's just over there."

Peter followed his brother's nod with his eyes. Across the ballroom, he encountered the truest cerulean eyes locked on his, and what little breath he had left was stolen away by her beauty. As his vision tunneled, Peter, the man, crossed the void to his waiting beloved and the realization of every good thing. Shoulders erect, steps confident, his carriage was that of a man eager to embrace his destiny.

8

Across the Ballroom

It took all Wendy's composure not to look about her in an effort to find Peter. For once, Aunt Mildred's instructions proved useful as Wendy made a grand display of being composed and charming. Inside, she was the complete opposite of her façade. Her brain whirled, her stomach churned, and her blood boiled. Her agitation was such that she could pay scarce attention to the conversation before her. Everything around her seemed so trivial. All that mattered—indeed, the only thing that mattered—was Peter.

She heard herself politely speaking about the weather, but the voice seemed to be coming from someone else. Then the voice, that came from her but was not hers, stopped mid-sentence. Across the room, the most intense, unnerving emerald eyes were boring into her soul.

The sight of Peter in his tuxedo was breathtaking! Wendy's knees began to knock, and she grasped a nearby chair for support. Everything that unfolded after, to Wendy, seemed to happen in slow motion.

With single-mindedness, Peter most deliberately crossed the floor toward her. His intense eyes devoured her from the inside out. The closer he came, the more disoriented she felt. Sure she was about to swoon, Wendy looked away.

Peter came to a stop directly in front of her, but she dared not look at him, fixing her eyes, instead, to a spot on the marble floor. He quietly cleared his throat to gain her attention, but still, she could not look up.

"Miss Darling." His deep voice caused her heart to rise to her mouth. "Allow me to introduce myself. I am Peter Neverland." Bending forward, he took her hand from her side, his touch fire to her clammy skin.

Raising her ungloved hand reverently to his lips, Peter kissed her.

To kiss a lady's hand was perfectly acceptable and chaste, and yet Wendy's blood raced with the intimacy of the action. Her skin radiated with warmth and remembrance, as if this was not its first meeting with Peter's touch. Her eyes flashed to his. "I know who you are, Sir," she replied more harshly than intended.

Undeterred, Peter beamed at her. His smile conveyed the radiance of a thousand suns. "A waltz," he uttered in delight. "May I have this dance, Miss Darling?"

Without waiting for her response—for he had no doubt her answer would be anything other than *yes*—Peter pulled her to him. His free hand encircled her waist finding precise purchase against the swell of her hip. His rough jaw rasped against her cheek as he nuzzled her temple. In this way, Peter began to lead Wendy, waltzing in bold, carefree steps. They were the first to dance, but other couples soon filled the space around them until the floor swirled with graceful motion. Peter, however, was really the best dancer among them.

As Peter and Wendy danced, their senses became occupied with one another. One dance led to another and then another. Their ignorance of anything but each other gave them one glad hour, and as it was to be their last happy hour for some time, let us rejoice that there were sixty glad minutes in it.

As Wendy twirled in the young actor's arms, something buried and long-forgotten stirred in her soul. A feeling or recollection of a similar experience from her childhood worked itself around in her brain. Innocent and heartless, it wanted to skip around the room for joy.

She almost knew him in that moment. In fact, if the very grown-up acting Wendy hadn't deliberately rejected her instincts as childish, she and Peter both might have been rescued from the resulting folly and we might have been spared a story. But she did not heed her lost child, and the events that consequently transpired were set into unalterable motion.

In the way a loose thread can unravel an entire jumper, sometimes the most inconsequential of events set into motion the beginning of the end. Wendy's thread was this: after several dances, the musicians took a well-earned break. Wendy, drunk with dancing, emerged from the golden sway of Peter's arms one sense at a time.

First, cool air on her cheek replaced the warm scrape of Peter's jaw. Then Peter released her form, which had so perfectly melded to his that the action created the sensation of one being cleaved in half. The scent of Peter—one of spicy, masculine possibility—was replaced with the pungency of food, and instead of gentle melodies, speculative babble assaulted her ears. Her eyes blinked open to discover Peter staring in rapture which caused her mouth to go dry. His gaze was so penetrating that she looked away and, in doing so, exchanged unfortunate glances with the iron scrutiny of Aunt Mildred.

The old woman, who had insisted on attending as Wendy's personal chaperone, had a distasteful look on her shrewd face as if she saw some unwelcome pest scurrying about the room. And understandably so, as the look on Wendy's face confirmed the old matriarch's suspicions about her niece's ulterior motives. In that moment, Wendy knew Aunt Mildred had guessed the truth.

Aunt Mildred was not the only person to have noticed Peter's particular attention. The whole room seemed to be abuzz with conjecture. The observation caused Wendy to focus on her external surroundings rather than the boy in front of her, who, even now, leaned in for a kiss.

Wendy stepped back causing Peter to halt mid-gesture. But unable to recognize her movements as reaction to his action and unwilling to let go of their moment, he advanced.

"Wendy," he implored so familiarly and tenderly. He still had enough boyish arrogance left in him to be thoughtless of anything but his most pressing need. Need of Wendy. Heedless of their audience, he reached out to stroke her cheek.

Conscious of Aunt Mildred closing in, Wendy began to panic. She flinched away from Peter's hand, her cheeks burning with shame. Perhaps, if she had not been from such good society, she wouldn't have cared that all eyes were on her. If she had had more to draw from in life, she might have been able to be coy and flirtatious. Maybe she could have matched Peter's stare and cunningly made some encouraging retort. Perhaps she could have even given Peter some indication that she returned his sentiments. Then, he would have escorted her to the garden where they could have privately declared the magnitude of their feelings for one another.

If only Peter, merely by being himself, had not stripped her to the point of transparency for the whole of London society to witness!

Instead, Wendy was ill equipped to deal with either the force of her internal emotions or the external scrutiny. With Aunt Mildred bearing down on her and the entire ballroom gawking with unveiled curiosity, the poor girl did the only thing in her nature to do. She fled.

"Please, do excuse me," she mumbled. Then, she turned her back to and walked away from the only thing that truly mattered to her. It took every ounce of effort to get through the front doors and outside without breaking into a run. Once escaped, however, Wendy Darling ran all the way home.

Only when she had locked herself in her room did she allow her insides to explode outward in gut-wrenching sobs. Hours later, although exhausted, Wendy could not sleep. What must Peter think of her? How could she ever explain to him when she didn't understand herself? Surely Aunt Mildred would inform Wendy's parents of her secret; how would she ever make them understand? They would never forgive their daughter for loving an actor when a banker was within her grasp.

We must not be too severe with Wendy, whose life had not been her own since childhood. The rich matriarchs who ruled her class still clung to the notion that a favorable match was indeed the only situation that could deliver a young lady from financial and societal ruin. Such matches were measured by bank accounts, not sentiments. When it came to the Darling household, venerable Aunt Mildred was no different.

Near daybreak, Wendy began to doze. In her dreams, the brave Wendy accompanied her to the party, lending her strength. When finally face to face with Peter, everything went exactly as it should. Peter escorted her to the garden where he professed his love. How her heart leapt for joy! Wendy was about to make her own declaration when cutthroat pirates descended upon them from all sides. They were a horrible lot of the blackest villains with ropes and knives.

Peter leapt forward to protect her. Taking on a dozen at once, he fought valiantly, but it was no use. They were captured. As they were being taken to the Pirate Captain, a little glowing light appeared. At first, she thought the mischievous pixie was there to save them. As it got closer,

Wendy realized that it was tinkling with glee. The spiteful creature was laughing because it had led the pirates to the garden. It had orchestrated their capture.

With growing horror, Wendy realized the satisfied pixie was not laughing merely because of what had occurred but because of the terrible things the pirates had yet in store for her...

Peter's eyes popped open and blinked rapidly to dispel his nightmare.

He'd been dreaming horrible dreams. Profoundly disturbed, he'd stayed up most of the night dissecting the ball over and over in an effort to figure out how the evening had gone so terribly wrong. In retrospect, his sentiments had seemed an embarrassment to Wendy. Not only did she not return his feelings, but also, as her good aunt explained, she had come in hopes of encountering another. Had she only danced with him out of charity? The thought that she would be ashamed of him had never crossed his mind. That is until Wendy fled and her most apologetic aunt had had the decency to explain the way of things.

"My good Sir," the Grand Dame had said as she halted him from going after the girl of his dreams. "I feel I must apologize. My niece has an unusual sense of propriety and is easily offended."

Peter, while concerned as to Wendy's flight, scoffed at this. "Surely, I am not the cause of any offense." It is humiliating to have to confess that this conceit of Peter was one of his most fascinating qualities.

"By no means..." the good matriarch replied. "However, tongues do tend to wag. Sometimes, sentiments are better handled in private, do you not agree?"

Peter took her to mean that he should have escorted Wendy to the garden before trying for a kiss and that this breach of propriety alone had been the source of Wendy's mortification. "Of course. I should go apologize."

Quick as a cobra strike the old woman placed a deterring hand on Peter's arm. "Perhaps it would be better if I speak with her. For I am confident if anyone can make her see sense, it is I."

He was ever so grateful Wendy's good aunt had come along as chaperone. With her to champion his cause, Peter felt sure his beloved would be persuaded to hear him out. Feeling nothing more than mild agitation, he paced the foyer, awaiting Aunt Mildred and Wendy's return.

The unfortunate boy had no way of discerning that he had placed his faith in the most deceitful of champions. Aunt Mildred, it must be said, did follow her niece outside. And that is where her pursuit ended. Under the guise of taking air, she tarried and happened to overhear the most fortuitous of conversations between the theatre company's director and its producer regarding an invitation to perform in New York and a shortage of funding. To ensure the troupe's swift departure to America, the Grand Dame pledged a most sizeable donation in exchange for a guarantee of anonymity.

After an appropriate length of time, Aunt Mildred reentered the ball to find Peter. She claimed Wendy had made to her a startling confession (which she would only recount to Peter after much coaxing).

"It seems my niece is an ambitious girl. She's informed me that her sights are set on a most eligible young banker, and it would not do for gossip to undermine her careful plotting. Why she only agreed to attend the ball in hopes of encountering the young gentleman. As he was not here, not even my urging could convince her to stay. She has asked me to implore you to respect her wishes by never speaking to her again."

Peter could hardly believe the enraptured theatre patron, his Wendy, regarded another above him. When they danced, he'd felt assured that her heart mirrored his own in sentiment. However, if his love wanted him to leave her alone, then he would attempt to comply and never see her again.

It was actually a relief when Mr. Frohman's big announcement came with such fortunate timing. Thanks to a very generous donation, he was taking the entire company to America to present *The Three Musketeers* on the New York stage.

They would leave in two weeks' time on the *Lusitania*. For the heartbroken Peter, it would not be soon enough. Therefore, he volunteered to go over early with Mr. Frohman and Mr. Boucicault. They would leave in three days for Fishguard, Wales and from there take the *Mauretania* to New York. Peter was not sure even putting an ocean between Wendy and himself would ease his heartbreak...but he had to try.

As he began to pack, he reflected on his disturbing sleep. In his dreams, Wendy had returned his love and at the ball, he had swept her off her feet and into the garden where the two could be alone. *He had been staring into her lovely blue eyes, leaning in, about to kiss her perfect mouth...when, from out of nowhere, appeared the vilest lot of murderous pirates led by his little dream guide.*

Instantly, he knew they meant Wendy harm! He fought as hard as he could but he was no match for them. The pirates strung them up to take back to their Captain. Bound and gagged, Peter could only listen to the horrible things they had planned for his beloved Wendy.

Three Days After the Party

Peter and Wendy hovered together in mid-air above a lovely forest alive with twinkling lights. The night was magical; shining stars above and shimmering fairies below. Face-to-face, they were both dancing and floating at the same time. Twirling with his beloved in his arms, Peter could feel her smooth skin beneath his touch; he could smell her lilac scented hair; sense her sweet breath on his cheek. He leaned in to kiss her. Her lips were warm, soft and welcoming. A perfect kiss that seemed to last for a long time.

When they finally pulled apart, the fairies were gone. Dark, stormy clouds hid the stars as heavy drops of rain began to fall. A bolt of lightning pierced the sky right between the lovers. The force of the blast ripped them apart, sending them in opposite directions.

As Peter tumbled backward through the darkness, he lost sight of Wendy. Crashing into the churning sea, the whole world went round and gray and wet. Trying not to panic, he let an air bubble escape from his lips and followed it until his head broke through the surface of the turbulent water. There was no land to be seen and Wendy was gone. In vain he called to her, "Wendy! Wendy!"

Somehow, he knew their situation was hopeless. Although sure she had also been cast into the sea, he was certain she was on the far side of the island. With effort compounded by fatigue and the heavy futility of the situation, he began to swim to her. He would find Wendy or die trying...

Soaking wet and twisted in his bedclothes, Peter awoke from his sleep, shaken. His lips tasted of salt and the cloying scent of seaweed clogged his nose. Muscles shaking, he pulled himself out of bed and dressed with effort in the darkness. It was nearly morning, and he still had one thing to do before he left.

Leaving a note for Griffin, he made his way to Wendy's cobbled street. This was not the first time he had stood outside No. 14, although it might very well be the last. Despite the chill in the air her window was wide open, as if expecting a visitor. As he had many times before, Peter wished he could fly up to her windowsill and watch her sleep. Desperately, he wanted to behold her perfect face one final time before he departed.

Standing in the predawn quiet, Peter wondered if it were feasible to steal across the garden and scale the trellis nearest her window. Still, if Wendy wanted nothing to do with him, he would not chance her waking to find him staring in at her. How wonderful, he thought, it would be to have a cloak of invisibility, to be able to see his beloved without the risk of causing her more distress.

"Peter..."

Peter flinched as a faint noise came drifting down to him from

Wendy's window. He could not be certain, but it sounded as if she'd said his name. Did Wendy know he was there? Was she calling to him? Every muscle tensed. He pressed against the high bars of the garden gate straining to listen. He remained that way, motionless and fierce in concentration, until the morning sun began to paint its colors across the Eastern sky.

In the distance, a cock began to crow, the faint chiming of Big Ben joining its morning song. In an hour, he would be on a train to Wales and, by nightfall, aboard a ship bound for America. He had yet to say his goodbyes to Griffin and Father. It was time to go.

Peter's body felt too cold and leaden to move. In spite of Wendy's revelation of a rival at the party, he hadn't completely surrendered hope of pursuing her. Therefore, the afternoon after the ball he had made his way to the very same spot. Then, not knowing what else to do, he called out to his beloved in a bold and brazen way that caused the curtains of every neighbor to part with curiosity.

"Wendy!"

He only had to shout for a moment before he was admitted into the Darling household. As fate would have it, Wendy's good aunt had been in residence. In the very drawing room of No. 14, Wendy's Aunt Mildred had amiably received him and, under the continued guise of a caring Grand Dame, sealed his fate.

"Mr. Neverland," she upbraided. "Hollering from the street! Surely you are not so vindictive as to bring scandal to my niece. If you truly care for her as you say, you would not injure her such."

"I would never injure, Miss Darling!" Peter protested. "If only I could speak with her, I am certain we could clear the matter up to your satisfaction."

The old spinster laid a gnarled hand against her breast. "My satisfac-

tion, my fine young actor? I have no fault with you. Indeed, I think you would be good for my niece." The woman heaved a martyr's sigh. "Heaven knows how I have championed your cause. Even the inferiority of your station would not be an obstacle, if I believed she truly loved you. But she does not. With all my heart, I did not wish to impart to you that which I now must." Slipping a piece of parchment out of her skirt pocket, she explained, "This was written by my niece's own hand."

Opening the letter, Peter scanned the few lines intended to repulse him, his face clouding with each word. It was Wendy's handwriting, for it matched the elegant script of her R.S.V.P. perfectly. (It would do us well, at this juncture, to remember by whose hand the reply to Mr. Frohman's grand ball had been issued.) In accordance with Peter's very nature, it never occurred to him to doubt the authenticity of either document. He had no experience with persons who, under the guise of respectable advice, forged letters and manipulated others into doing their will. The elders in his own life were forthright, the very pillars of integrity. So we cannot fault him for what he did not yet know. Peter would learn of life's deceit soon enough.

We will not recount the message other than to say it was most ruthless and unforgiving in its sentiments. Words, after all, are merely scribbles of ink on parchment. Even hurtful words are neither sticks nor stones. What is important to note, is the letter achieved its desired effect.

Rigidly, Peter refolded the paper and handed it back to the sympathetic Grand Dame. "If this is how Miss Darling feels," he said stiffly. "I shan't trouble her any further. Please tell your niece I shall never bother her again."

Poor Peter! He had no way to discern such flagrant lies. In that moment, the remaining vestiges of his boyhood conceit were crushed.

Now as the cock heralded the rosy predawn over the London skies, Peter took one last look at the open window and let two great tears escape down his cheeks. His shattered heart had not yet hardened in the wake of life's cruel lesson. And try as he might, he could not hate she whom just days before he adored with his whole being.

He wanted to shout, *"I will always love you! I will never be the same without you!"* Instead, he clenched his eyes shut and whispered, "Good-bye, Wendy." Full of regret, he hurried through the waking streets with every intention never to return.

Wendy was being tossed to and fro. She had lost track of how much time had elapsed since the storm had ripped her from Peter's strong arms and flung her into the cruel sea. She had called his name with all her strength. "Peter! Peter!" But he was gone. The rolling waves were growing more violent, filling her mouth and nose in a relentless assault. Her body burned with the effort of trying to keep her head above water, but she would not surrender. As long as Peter was coming for her, she would continue to fight-until her last breath.

The next wave crashed over her with violent force, and for one disorienting moment, the whole world was liquid. As she surfaced, choking on salt water, Wendy thought for the first time that Peter might not be coming to her rescue. Another wave engulfed her, but the sea mattered little in the face of Peter's abandonment. Drowning in despair, she knew she would not last long alone...

"Wendy, wake up!"

Disoriented, soaking wet, and tangled in her bed linens, she was being vigorously shaken from side to side. Having been in bed for three days, ever since she returned from the ball, it took Wendy a moment to realize she was not experiencing another horrifying dream. She opened her eyes, relieved she was not being accosted by waves again but by her dear friend, Maimie.

"Wendy, wake up! I have been telephoning for hours. You look terrible! You're drenched. Are you ill?" Although invited, Maimie, swamped with wedding arrangements, had not been able to attend Mr. Frohman's Ball. In fact, she had not spoken with Wendy since the day their invitations arrived.

Wendy pulled her bed sheets over her head in self-pity. "I'm dying, Maimie. Just let me be."

Vexed, Wendy's dearest friend yanked back the covers. "What is happening? I go to Perrin Hall for a fortnight to make wedding preparations and everything goes to pieces in my absence. Even you! I had anticipated returning to find you in a state of sublime bliss. Instead, you are dying, and the entire company of *The Three Musketeers* is headed to America."

The shock of her friend's revelation caused Wendy to bolt out of bed. "Peter is leaving?" she cried.

Maimie took her friend gently by the shoulders. "Peter is gone...hadn't you heard? He leaves for New York tonight on the *Mauretania*. He is already en route to Wales."

Poor Wendy! If only she had known how close Peter had been in the last few days—in her parlor, below her very window—perhaps she could have summoned the courage to follow her heart. To speak to him and explain why she panicked.

So what if her aunt disapproved? Why should Wendy care if Aunt Mildred's bank account ruled their household? She should have risked everything for love—for Peter!

Sometime in her past, she felt sure she'd been a much braver Wendy. If only she could go back in time to find herself and ask the brave Wendy what to do.

She sank to the edge of her bed, shivering uncontrollably. "Maimie, he cannot go! What will I do without him? How will I continue to exist?"

In the end, it was the courage of her dearest friend that lent her strength. "Go to him," Maimie urged sitting and wrapping her arm around Wendy's damp shoulders. "Or better yet, go with him!"

Wendy shook her head negatively. "What would I say to him?"

"What is in your heart?"

"Love."

"Then say that. What else really matters?"

Wendy regarded her dearest friend longingly. "Oh Maimie, if only—"

"If only *what*? We can catch him in Wales. My parents are away in the country. I have their motorcar and driver downstairs. I have already told your mother and aunt that I require your assistance at Perrin Hall. But if we are to do this thing, we must leave now. This very instant!"

Wendy did not waste time on words. She jumped up from her bed, grabbed her slippers, wrapped a shawl around her nightgown, and headed for the waiting motorcar. Maimie could scarcely keep up.

Apart from leaving Wendy, saying goodbye to Griffin was the hardest thing Peter had done in his young life. Although his brother would have accompanied him to Fishguard, Peter insisted they say their farewells at Paddington Station. In return, Griffin had insisted on carrying his brother's bags the entire way.

When the time came, the brothers, who never lacked for conversation, struggled for words.

"Griffin?"

"Aye, Peter?"

"Take care of Father."

"Aye, Peter."

"I am not sure that he really understands…"

"He understands you better than you think. And he loves you."

"You and Father are the world to me."

"Aye, Peter."

The train whistled.

"Griffin?"

"Aye, Peter."

"Will you promise to do something for me?"

"Anything."

"Go to the matinee each Saturday. Write to me about her."

"Aye, Peter."

The brothers hugged until the train whistled again and began to move. Peter jumped aboard, and Griffin handed him his bags. Then each man remained motionless, watching until the other was out of sight.

There was nothing to do on the long drive to Wales but talk, so that is what Wendy and Maimie did. Wendy had insisted her friend go first. So Maimie, sensing her listener's fragile emotional state, prattled on for hours, breaking the wedding down into the most trivial of details.

It was only after their driver announced that they were nearing Fishguard, that Wendy dared recount to her friend the events of three days past. The entire trip Wendy had been ordering pieces in her mind as if completing a puzzle. The last piece was fitting into place even now, as she spoke. After the disastrous party, Wendy's family had been all too compliant with her wishes to be left alone. They had asked no questions of her. In fact, they had made no demands of her at all except that she submit to an examination by the family physician. Dr. Trimble had promptly inspected her and diagnosed extreme fatigue. He prescribed a week of bed rest and gave her some pills to help her sleep. Under her aunt's meticulous ministrations, she'd been sleeping on and off since.

Maimie was horrified. "Do you think Aunt Mildred conspired with the doctor to keep you in bed until Peter had gone?"

"Maimie, I am sure of it! She assumed my care with such pity and thoroughness, and all she really wanted was to keep me drugged. I knew when she said nothing of the ball that something was amiss! I thought perhaps she had taken sympathy on my plight. I imagined that she had recognized the truth of my love and that truth had melted her heart. I wrongly assumed that she was on my side when all along she was merely protecting her family interests."

"Hateful, old cow!"

"A cow is too much a compliment!" Wendy spat. "She is a venomous serpent! I shan't underestimate her again."

The automobile began to slow. Maimie opened the front window to address her driver. "Giles, are we there?"

"Close, Miss."

"Why have we slowed?"

"There is too much traffic, Miss. Everyone is trying to get to the port, and the streets are clogged. Look."

The girls looked in the direction indicated by their driver. In the distance was the sea, and on it a great ship with billowing smokestacks. As they watched, its horn bellowed, and the crewman began to take up its gangplanks. Maimie groaned. The ground between the ship and their car was a sea of a different kind, an impassable sea of humanity.

The driver looked at Wendy. "If you're going to catch that ship you are going to have to make a run for it, Miss."

In unison, Wendy and Maimie bolted from the car. Running as fast as the situation allowed, they wove and pushed their way thru the living sea to get to the ship. All around them, people were stationary and yet moving at the same time. Some cheering, some crying, all were waving toward the massive vessel and shouting "Bon voyage!" The entire ship undulated as those departing waved their last goodbyes back to the crowd.

When they finally reached the gate, a surly crewman stopped their progress. Maimie tried to reason with him while Wendy scanned the decks searching for some sign of Peter. Wendy was a sight! Still in her nightdress and slippers, shawl clutched around her shoulders and her loose hair whipped about by the harsh December wind, she looked like an escaped lunatic.

Perhaps if she had looked more presentable, the girls would have been able to make headway with the apathetic crewman. When it was apparent that he was not going to yield, Wendy hurried down a length of the pier scanning the departing passengers frantically. She saw Mr. Boucicault and recognized the backside of Mr. Frohman as he departed from the upper deck. But where was Peter?

In vain, she tried to yell and attract their attention, but her cries blended with the voices of those surrounding her. Wendy knew her only hope was to separate herself from this horde of rippling humanity. As the ship began to move, Wendy pushed her way back up the pier, through the mass of people, toward the rocky beach. Gingerly, she made her way out across the jagged jetty. Arms raised over her head and flailing, wind tugging at her hair and nightgown, she seemed more specter than woman.

Many aboard the ship noticed the desperate girl who was precariously waving from atop the rocks; speculation about who she was and her intent became a regular topic of dining room gossip during the voyage. While most people had differing opinions on her purpose, it was generally agreed that she made a most tragic figure. Like Catherine on the moors, the strange girl seemed to be searching in vain for her Heathcliff.

"The party's on the other side of the ship, M'boy!" Mr. Frohman snuck up on Peter, who had found himself a deserted piece of deck on the opposite side of the ship from the harbor.

Peter had been reflecting on his latest dream. Maybe it was an omen. Perhaps it meant the ship would founder or be set upon by pirates, if such a thing still existed. Neither scenario bothered him terribly much. As Mr. Frohman approached, Peter had been vividly imagining a siege by a great pirate ship complete with skull and bones and a neurotic, one-handed Captain.

"I am not really in the mood for a party, Sir." He had been in a bleak mood ever since he had woken up. The cold winter sky and gray churning ocean seemed to echo his feelings.

"Do you want to talk about it, son?"

Peter regarded the older man for a moment then shaking his head walked over to the railing. "Not really, no."

The American joined him at the rail and for many moments they stared out at the vast expanse of ocean in contemplative silence.

"Is this your first crossing, Peter?"

"Yes, Sir."

The older man's eyes twinkled. "I was aboard the *Lusitania* in October of nineteen-o-seven when she broke the eastbound record and got the Blue Riband. Ah, I shall never forget that fantastic crossing! I have never crossed on the *Mauretania* before." He chuckled. "I almost feel unfaithful! I shall have to be on my guard with Old Lusie, lest she try to get even with me for cheating on her with her sister."

Dion Boucicault joined them then. "There you chaps are! You do know that the party is on the other side of the ship? Look here, I managed to save some champagne for you. And not just any champagne! This is from Prince Radziwell's private collection. Did you hear we had a couple of princes aboard? They are both quite capital fellows!"

Mr. Boucicault produced an unopened bottle, which he promptly handed off to Mr. Frohman, and three crystal glasses. Charles Frohman popped the cork and poured them each a drink.

"Now then boys," inquired the American producer as he set the nearly empty bottle on a deck chair. "What shall we toast to?"

"You chaps missed a curious sight in the harbour," Boucicault interjected. "A young woman, in what looked to be her nightdress, standing alone on the rocks frantically waving at the ship. Her blonde tresses whipping about her most dramatically."

At the mention of a nightdress, Peter's heart gave a start. "Was she a lady?"

"From the look of her, I'd say not. Still, she seemed a most noble and tragic figure. Like Isolde or Juliet. It is to her that I would like to toast. May the fine lady find what she was looking for or may she be able to start anew... To the blessing of new beginnings!"

"To new beginning!"

"To new beginnings!"

Peter toasted, wanting to believe with his whole heart. But something inside of him, tenacious and petulant, as obstinate as a child, dug in its heels and refused to let go.

10
An Ocean Away

Peter dreamed of a dense forest. Something was falling from the sky. It was a beautiful white bird. He began to run, straining to get to the spot where the bird would land. He could hear it crashing through the brush in front of him.

Up ahead was a small clearing, and he glimpsed the pitiful creature lying prostrate on the ground, unmoving. As he came closer, he saw the bird had long blonde tresses, delicate hands, and little feet. It was not a white bird at all but a girl in a nightgown. Sticking out of her breast was the shaft of an arrow.

She appeared to be dead. Her head was facing away from him, so it was not until he circled round the girl that he realized she was familiar to him. Heart hitching painfully in his chest, he realized the motionless girl was a younger version of his Wendy.

A groan escaped from Peters lips. Frenzied he looked about him for the archer who had delivered Wendy's fatal blow. In his shock, he was barely conscious of grasping something in his hands; he looked down as if in slow motion and saw he held a bow. With horror he realized that his own hands were responsible for Wendy's fate. Peter had shot the Wendy bird.

Traversing the Atlantic was not the cathartic experience that Peter had hoped it would be. New York, particularly Broadway, was an exciting, exotic place and Peter did his best to immerse himself in the hustle and bustle. Everything, however, seemed to remind him of she whom he was trying to forget. Each time something would delight him, his immediate thought would be of Wendy and her imagined reaction.

Every night Peter still dreamt of her. Often there were strange islands surrounded by rough seas, frequently there were murderous pirates, sometimes there were strange boys, occasionally he encountered Indians or Mermaids, sporadically his dream guide still appeared, and always there was the separation. Sometimes he would wake up with her name on his lips, exhausted from spending the whole night searching for Wendy in a strange netherworld. No matter what he tried, he could not control the dreams nor stop them from coming.

So, Peter threw himself into his work; and being a young, handsome actor, the American public in return, threw itself at him. Within six months of his arrival, there was an endless amount of ladies wanting to make Peter Neverland's acquaintance, among other things. These women were everywhere. They stalked the alley behind the stage door, bribed their way into his dressing and hotel rooms, even staked out his favorite restaurants. The better-connected and moneyed ones, under the guise of patronage, hosted dinners and organized parties. Peter, of course, was always the esteemed guest of honor.

Despite being offered every manor of lavish gift including physical charms, Peter delicately refused them all. He still wanted that which was an ocean away. Without being able to help himself, he compared each woman he met to Wendy and found them all wanting...

Still heavy with melancholy from his latest dream, Peter walked through the newly renamed Belasco Theatre. He moved reverently, pausing to admire the beautiful George Keister architecture, the opulent Tiffany glasswork, and the lively murals by Everett Shinn. This theatre had been his closest thing to an actual home for the last six months, and he adored it.

In the approaching evening, the building was uncharacteristically still. Peter's company had packed earlier in the day—they would be leaving for Chicago in the morning—thus the theatre was dark. As Peter moved through the stillness, he wondered why he had been summoned to the Bishop's residence above.

The designer and namesake of the theatre, David Belasco, was considered an innovative eccentric among the American Theatre world. His insistence on clerical garb, a black suit with white rounded collar, had earned him the nickname "the Bishop of Broadway." Peter, whose very nature was to be charitable in spirit and mind, supposed all-encompassing passion for the theatre was a religious calling of sorts and respected the man for his devotion.

Mr. Belasco, perhaps recognizing a fellow devotee, had been trying to entice Peter away from his company with a series of appealing offers, but the actor had made it clear that he had committed to the run of Musketeers in Chicago. Afterwards, Peter thought, was quite a different story. Although he hadn't informed them, Peter never intended to return with his fellow thespians to London. It was too near his pain, too near his heart and her.

Eventually, Peter made his way to the Bishop's apartment high atop the east side of the building. The formidable man was waiting for him at the door. In anticipation of yet another flattering offer, Peter stepped into the Bishop's chambers clearing his throat.

"Mr. Belasco," he began.

"David," corrected the Bishop.

"David, your offers flatter me, but..."

"Sit down, son." The Bishop gestured to a chair.

Peter seated himself. Something in the faux cleric's face divulged that this meeting had nothing to do with any previous offers.

"Peter, this arrived for you, care of the theatre, this morning." He handed him a slip of paper. "I'll give you a few minutes." Then the Bishop was gone.

Peter turned the telegram over and over in his hands, afraid to open it. His first thought, however improbable, was that it was from Wendy; then he worried that it was about her. Deciding it was probably no cause for alarm, he reluctantly opened it. It was from Griffin.

DEAR PETER. I AM SORRY TO INFORM YOU THAT FATHER HAS PASSED AWAY. AT HIS REQUEST THERE WILL NOT BE A FUNERAL. PLEASE DO NOT COME HOME. CONTINUE WITH YOUR PERFORMANCES. LETTER TO FOLLOW WILL EXPLAIN ALL. GRIFFIN.

Peter was not sure how long he sat, but he was in complete darkness when the Bishop returned with a drink for each of them. Later, stunned and slightly drunk, he returned to his hotel room where a grinning bellhop informed him that a certain well-known actress was waiting in his private rooms. For the first time since his arrival in America, Peter did not turn a female admirer away; in fact, she did not leave until morning.

At this point, we must take caution to not be hasty to judge Peter by virtue of a closed door and a sunrise. Appearances, after all, are seldom as they seem. Peter was a gentleman of the highest moral caliber. This, above all else, is to be remembered.

If only the loose-tongued bellhop would have given Peter the same benefit of the doubt instead of jumping to scandal-sized conclusions...

An ocean away, Wendy was tired of her dreams; waiting for Peter, wanting Peter, searching for Peter, screaming for Peter, hating Peter for leaving her. Every night the darkness pressed in around her. Terrible, evil forces divided her from her love and threatened them harm. She thought she was going mad!

Seven months had passed since the handsome, young actor had left for America. At first, Wendy didn't want to go on living. She shut herself in her room and barely got out of bed. At Aunt Mildred's insistence and for fear of driving Wendy into the actor's arms, her family indulged her.

Successfully, she cut herself off from nearly everyone and everything. Despite her best efforts, she had only two faithful visitors: Maimie, whom she admitted; and James, whom she did not.

Like clockwork, Maimie arrived on Saturday afternoon. For Wendy's benefit, she brought the daily and weekly papers already scoured for any mention of Peter or his company. This particular Saturday, she entered Wendy's room with less sympathy and more purpose. In her hands, she held a beautiful summer hat, which she proceeded to thrust at Wendy.

"Wendy, get dressed!" she ordered. "I am taking you to tea."

Wendy set the hat on the edge of the bed and tightened her robe around her thin frame. "Oh Maimie, I am not inclined to leave the house today. I already arranged to have tea brought up."

"Nonsense!" Her companion crossed to the window, parted the curtains, and opened it. "You haven't left the house in months. It is a beautiful day! Today, we are going out."

Indignantly, Wendy opened her mouth in offence. "I get out! I went to your wedding," Wendy snapped. Fancy Wendy snapping! But she had been much tried, and she little knew what loyal service her dearest friend would perform on behalf of her broken heart. If she had known, she would not have snapped.

Maimie's gaze cut her short, and Wendy's eyes dropped to a spot on the rug. Her best friend and confidant came closer. Reproachfully, Maimie picked up the hat and held it out to her. "That was one time. One time in seven months, and you didn't even dance."

"I didn't *feel* like it," she mumbled accepting the beautiful millinery.

"I do not think you *feel* at all. Whatever you are doing, you are certainly not alive. Now, get dressed. Today, you rejoin the living."

Wendy looked skeptically at her bosom companion and sank to the edge of her bed. The latter picked her back up and tenderly smoothed a wisp of hair away from her face.

"It is just tea, dearest. I'm not asking you to throw a party!"

Sensing that her dear friend was not about to yield, Wendy began to dress. The ritual of dressing seemed strange after so many months of apathy. It occurred to Wendy that the whole point of clothes—from hair combs, to corset, to boots—was to transform a woman into something contradictory to her natural state. At the same time, there was something cathartic and calming in those same ministrations. For the better part of an hour, Maimie helped her dress. By the time she was finished, Wendy was surprised to realize that she was actually looking forward to leaving her house.

Seated at the best table in the most fashionable tea shoppe in all of London, Wendy felt lighter than she had in a long time. She smiled at her faithful friend. "Oh, I didn't realize how much I missed this."

"And I missed you! Nothing is the same without you."

"Have you been to the theatre recently?"

Maimie frowned, shaking her head, "No, the Opera."

Wendy mirrored the expression. "Oh dear."

"Oh dear, indeed!"

The friends began to laugh like old times. When a dour grand-dame and her unfortunate looking daughter passed by casting the pair reproachful glances, Maimie responded with a snort. Then they giggled like schoolgirls until their cheeks ached and tears were streaming from their eyes. In those precious moments all Wendy's pent-up emotions were released.

After a bit, when things had calmed down, Wendy glanced expectantly at a small stack of newspapers folded under Maimie's handbag.

"What news of Peter?"

"Well," Maimie hesitated, "the company has moved on to Chicago. Last week, in fact."

Wendy sensed her friend's reluctance. "What else?"

Maimie placed her hand over her companion's. "Are you sure you want to know?" Wendy's somber nod prompted her to continue in careful words. "It seems Peter has been linked to a well-known actress."

Wendy pulled back her hand as if stung. "Who?" She demanded.

Maimie exhaled and pulled out the small stack of papers. "Edith Wynne Matthison."

"And what do you mean by 'linked'?"

"It seems she spent the night in his hotel room."

Wendy snatched the papers from her friend's hand and read the accounts for herself. (This was still a couple of years before the scandal between Edith and the pretty Vassar coed that would have dispelled any gossip about her and a member of the opposite sex.) After reading, Wendy was silent for a long time. When she finally looked at Maimie, her face was deliberately blank.

"Well, he's found someone, at long last." She smiled a pitiful smile. "Good for him."

Her friend was not so accepting. "More like someone found him. For Heaven's sake, she's married! It's nothing more than a tawdry affair."

"It doesn't matter." Wendy folded up the papers.

"Of course, it does! You could still go after him. The *Lusitania* leaves tomorrow for—"

"No, Maimie!" Now it was Wendy's turn to be firm. "It doesn't matter because I have decided to face the facts and move on. Peter is not coming back. He has made a new life for himself and I have to do the same."

Later that day James called upon her, flowers in hand, for his weekly visit. For the first time since Peter's departure, Wendy did not refuse him.

That night, as Wendy slept, a boy dressed in leaves flew into her room. She awoke to find him seated at the foot of her bed. Although he was unknown to her, he was at the same time familiar.

"Boy, what do you want?" she asked.

"For you." He held out his hand, and she took his offering. It was an acorn button.

She took his gift and placed it on a small silver chain, which she fashioned around her neck. "Thank you."

The boy grasped her hand and began to draw her toward the open window.

"Come away, Wendy."

How she longed to go with him. Somehow, she knew he could take her to a place where all her adult heartbreak would melt away and vanish like spun sugar. The boy released his grip and glided out the window. Floating in the air, he turned in a graceful loop and looked at her expectantly, a dimpled smile lighting his face.

"Come away, Wendy."

Perched on the windowsill, arms stretched outward, she murmured, "I can't. I can't fly."

"I'll teach you," the boy said hovering in front of her.

His outstretched hand was just beyond her reach, so Wendy strained forward to grasp it. Struggling to maintain her balance, she wildly flailed her arms. The boy disappeared before her eyes, and Wendy began to fall toward the darkened garden far below. With all her strength, she hurled herself backwards. For a moment, she was suspended mid-air as her feet flew out from under her, then she landed on her bedroom floor with a jarring thud.

Disoriented, Wendy sat in stunned silence trying to figure out if she was awake or dreaming. She settled the matter by giving herself a strong pinch on her forearm, which hurt rather a lot but left no doubt that she was awake.

She stood uncertainly and went to the open window. The cloudless night, illuminated by a harvest moon, revealed many twinkling stars but no flying boy. She did not know whether she was relieved or disappointed that he was just another figment of her dreams. And yet...

She turned and walked slowly to her dressing table. Opening its drawer, she pulled out her neglected keepsake box. Inside were her thimbles, including the mysterious porcelain half. Gently pushing them aside, she pulled out a tarnished silver chain. Attached to the end was a faded acorn button.

Although she had had the necklace since she was a child, she could not recall where it had come from. She pulled the acorn out of the box and examined it in the moonlight. It had a jagged hole in the center as if something had pierced it violently. Running her finger across it, she wondered what had made the hole and why it didn't go all the way through.

Clasping the chain around her neck, the acorn fell against her breast. She placed her hand over it. Surely, it was a good luck charm—a talisman that would protect her from harm and keep her safe. *Maybe*, she thought, *it already has...*

AUTOMATIC
VAUDEVILLE
NEVERLAND

11

The Wild West

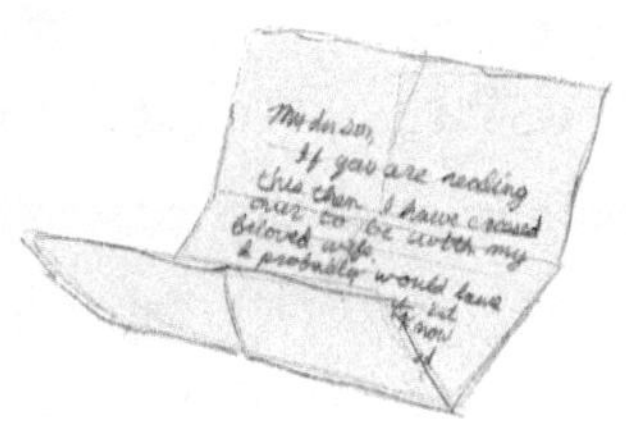

Odd things happen to all of us on our way through life without our noticing for a time that they have happened. Now such an experience had come that morning to Wendy as she contemplated her next visit from the young banker.

In truth, she was surprised by how much she actually enjoyed James's company. He was an attentive listener. A bit too reserved for her tastes, but nonetheless, his insights were remarkably thoughtful and mature. Although he lacked passion, he did love her in his quiet, faithful way. Above all, Wendy felt so sure of him; he would never hurt her nor abandon her. He would always put her above all else and with him her life would be safe.

So dread had evolved into anticipation and she received him—warmly.

But every so often when they were at tea or strolling in the park, James would get that familiar look in his eyes. The look that said, *I am ready to ask you the question, the most important thing a man can ask a woman. I am ready to be husband, father, and provider.*

Then in answer to James's eyes, Wendy would get a look of her own. Hers said, *Don't dare ask it! I am not yet ready.*

In those moments of unspoken communication, James and Wendy reached an understanding. Eventually she would marry him, so for now he would be patient and hold his tongue. Like the spring, their friendship progressed, with minor setbacks, but all in all developing slowly and steadily from a fragile shoot, cultivated in trust and dependability, growing until the day it would become a garden in full bloom.

It had been four months since she started seeing James and two since she had let him take her on outings. Saturday, they would join Lord and Lady Withington for the premier of George Bernard Shaw's *Misalliance* at the Duke of York's Theatre. This was the company's first production since their triumphant return from America minus Peter. All of London society, despite mourning the loss of its favorite young actor, was coming out to welcome them back. It was a first for Wendy too. Her first venture back to the theatre...back to Peter's world.

Despite the immense joy the theatre always afforded her, Wendy knew almost immediately that coming had been a mistake. However certain she was that Peter remained in America, she could not help but anxiously look for him in every direction she turned. Every person shadowed in the stage wings could have been him. Each scene change left her fretfully holding her breath in anticipation, waiting for his entrance. Might her intelligence be wrong? Perhaps Peter had changed his mind, returned to take his rightful place on the London stage and restore meaning to her precarious world. Hope was futile, yet it was not in Wendy's nature to do less.

Wishing aside, the play itself was painful—seeming to expose the fragile truce between her disappointed hopes and safer, more realistic, expectations. The subject, marriage for the wrong reasons, was too raw to heed, lest she begin to scrutinize the folly of her life and return to her bed indefinitely.

Uncomfortably seated in the Viscount's box rather than her accustomed seat in the dress circle, Wendy tried to think about other things until the final curtain descended. When the actors, Peter's friends and colleagues, took their final bows, their eyes seemed to hold silent accusations, as if they knew she was betraying him, and her heart, with James's company.

Please forgive me, she mutely begged.

A ripple in the curtain stage right caught her attention. Offstage, a young man was doing his best to spy on the audience without being seen. Wendy's heart slammed into her chest, and her breath hitched in her throat. For an instant, she believed it to be Peter. Then her vision grew acclimated to the shadows, and she realized the gentleman's coloring was too dark, his form too stocky, to be her heart's hope.

Before she could turn away in disappointment, the young man turned his penetrating chocolate eyes on her. Wendy froze under his scrutiny as he surveyed the boxes' occupants with a disapproving frown. To her dismay, James chose that exact moment to perform his duties as her escort, helping her from her seat and placing her wrap about her shoulders.

Taking James's arm, Wendy chanced a quick glace back toward the stage. The gentleman was still staring. His severe eyes fixed themselves on her, causing his countenance to darken even more. The hair on the back of her neck prickled unpleasantly, like when she had been caught in a lie as a child. Shivering, she ripped her eyes away and exited the theatre with her party.

In the lobby, she surreptitiously searched for the dark gentleman, both fearing and longing for an encounter. Somehow, albeit irrational, she felt certain that he was connected to Peter. After a moment, she saw him on the opposite side of the hall, making haste toward the exit, and her heart sank as she realized he was nearly gone. But as luck would have it, fate intervened on her behalf.

A dowager and her two young companions stopped the gentleman in his tracks. Wendy watched him blanch and then rearrange his features into a pleasant countenance. When not scowling in judgment, he was actually quite handsome to look at.

Wendy moved closer, so that she could respectably eavesdrop. However, the first word she overheard nearly caused her to give herself away. She pressed the back of her hand to her mouth to stifle a startled gasp. Whilst looking the other way, she inched closer, straining to hear what the older woman was asking about *Peter.*

"Aye," answered the young man, "Peter is still in America."

"And how does he care for it?" asked the more petulant of the two companions.

"A great deal, I believe. When he last wrote me from Chicago, he was headed west."

"Prospecting for gold?" asked the other girl in a high squeaky voice Wendy instantly disliked.

"Nay. Truth be told, I think he's trying to find himself."

"Why do you not urge him to come home, where he is known and loved by all?" It was the dowager who spoke.

"Nay, not all, Ma'am."

The gentleman's reply was so cryptic that Wendy dared a glance in his direction, only to find him looking pointedly at her. His eyes seemed to hold some sort of accusation that she could not fathom.

"Well, please tell your brother that the London stage is simply not the same without him." The dark-haired man nodded in reply as the grand lady, and her charges moved on.

Peter's brother?

Wendy realized that she was gaping at him open-mouthed like a carp and snapped her jaw shut. As soon as he was at liberty to do so, he returned his critical gaze to Wendy. She watched as the gentleman's brow furrowed again into a scowl. To her horror, he began to move toward her in measured purposeful steps. Her cheeks warmed as her blood rushed to her face.

Like a mouse caught in the pull of a mighty cobra, Wendy was mesmerized. As much as she wanted to flee, she was helpless to look away. In a half dozen steps, he would reach her. She had no idea what he wanted of her, but there was so much she wanted to ask of Peter's *brother.*

Then she heard James at her shoulder, his hand gently guiding her elbow. For the second time that night, she managed to rip herself away from those magnetic eyes and the spell was again broken. "A moment, James," was all she said. Feeling more herself, she turned back to confront Peter Neverland's brother, but to her astonishment, he was gone—vanished into thin air.

Not long ago. But how long ago? *It seemed to Wendy as if she had been flying for a long time. Surely, she could not still be over the Atlantic. How long ago had she decided to fly to America to track Peter down? Sometimes it was dark and sometimes light. At times she was very warm, but now, terribly cold...and sleepy. That was the danger—if she fell asleep, she would fall. She couldn't fly and sleep.*

Again it seemed to her that she ought to have reached America by now. Then Wendy had the loveliest of thoughts. Maybe Peter would fly out and meet her. Distracted, she started to nod off. As her chin touched her chest and the sensation of plummeting ripped through her, she jerked herself awake again. But she was so sleepy and still no land was to be seen. Looking with horror at the cruel sea far below, Wendy asked herself futilely, "How long?"

Wendy awoke exhausted; her arms aching. She supposed she had been thrashing about in her sleep again. No, not thrashing, but flying...

She had been flying across the Atlantic to find Peter. The imagery was crystal clear as if it had been an actual memory rather than a dream. Most of all, she remembered the torrid ocean waiting to swallow her up. If only Peter had come to rescue her. He had been out there also, flying just out of sight—she was certain of it. So why had he not come to her, when she had needed him so?

Could it be that he was just as lost as she?

Peter folded the well-worn letter and placed it hastily into his coat. Opening it had been habit, for he knew the contents by heart. The letter, written in his recently deceased father's hand, had caught up with him during his engagement in Chicago.

It read:

My Dear Son,

If you are reading this, then I have crossed over to be with my beloved wife.

I probably would have left this world long ago if it had not been for you and your brother. Know that you boys have given my life joy and meaning. Please do not mourn for me; I am ready to go.

I sometimes got the feeling you thought I was disappointed in you for not following in my footsteps. The truth is I could not have been prouder. I always understood that your path was to be different. From the moment I saw you, you reminded me of someone I knew when I was a boy. Someone, who found me when I was lost. Someone, I loved very much.

You and your brother have excelled as men. I hope you will be as happy and successful in your lives as I have been in mine. I wish you love, family, and the gift of risk. Bravely follow your heart!

To your brother, I leave our business. To you, Peter, I leave our home.

Your Ever Loving Father

Death was not an end. Peter felt it with every fiber in his being. They would meet again, and when they did, Peter would have the chance to vocalize all that was in his heart.

As to the living, Peter had written to Griffin insisting their home should belong to the elder brother as well. He had also taken the opportunity to convey the pride of kinship he felt toward his selfless brother.

In Griffin's penned reply, he simply said it would be his great honor to care for the house until the time Peter returned to claim it. And that he hoped Peter might return soon.

But rather than drawing closer to home, the young actor kept moving further away.

Checking his pocket watch, Peter hurried down Sunset Boulevard toward the set where they were to begin shooting on the morrow. The prospect of moving pictures was thrilling—so many new things to learn, to occupy his overactive mind—yet it had been hard to leave behind the company of players that had become his family. Harder still to know that they had resumed their rightful place on London's stage—front and center in Wendy's world.

Others had been difficult to leave as well; Edith Matthison, who had turned out to be a discreet and sympathetic ear, staying up the whole night in a purely sisterly way to talk when he had needed it the most; Charles and Dion who had treated him as equal despite their decades of theatrical experience; even David Belasco, the enigmatic Bishop of Broadway. The Bishop had come to see him one final time during their Chicago engagement, renewing his offer of patronage if Peter returned with him to New York.

When Peter graciously declined, the Bishop had asked, "Will you be going back to England then, son?"

"No, after I fulfill my Chicago contract, I am headed west. D.W. Griffith has offered me a role in his moving pictures venture."

The confusion and hurt had been clear in his would-be benefactor's eyes. "My dear boy, it is folly to leave the stage. Moving pictures will never amount to anything. Mark my words."

Of course the Bishop hadn't understood his refusal—Peter scarcely understood it himself. How could he admit that he was compelled to keep moving, always trying to stay one step ahead of his wasted heart? He tried his best never to think of Wendy, but even then she would not let go of him. Valiantly, he threw himself into his work, but when he stopped for any length of time, it was just as if she were inside him, knocking.

It would have been a wise stroke of self-preservation to ask Griffin to cease his news of Wendy—there seemed to be very little for his brother to report of late—however, the sparseness of information was the very reason he could not sever the tie. Each tidbit was precious, soothing the nagging questions in Peter's brain. Was she well? Was she happy? Was she cared for? Was she loved?

How he both desired and feared those answers!

Hastily he slipped his brother's latest correspondence from his pocket. It had arrived only this morning, and yet he had already read it a half a dozen times. Scanning the line that inflicted the most acute agony, Peter shut his eyes and returned the odious letter to its sheath. So Wendy had returned to the theatre...and with her young banker.

For months, Wendy had been absent from London society. His constant pestering had obliged Griffin to inquire after the lady directly through bribes to one of the Darling family servants. Peter had been relieved to learn she was at home and in good health. Information beyond that was a mystery. Dutifully, Griffin had confirmed Wendy's status each week, her health and withdrawal not changing. It gnawed at Peter, not knowing what circumstances kept his vivacious angel from the theatre. More than once, he had been tempted to return to England to try and discover the truth of it himself.

On those occasions, when tempted to give in, he had to remind himself that to Wendy Darling he mattered little, if at all. It would be folly to travel across the ocean for someone who did not care for him in the slightest. If only things had been different, nothing could have stopped him from hurrying to her side. But real life was not like a theatrical, only on the stage could a hero and heroine worlds apart come together as lovers and defy the odds for a happy ending.

"Peter!"

A demanding and distinctly feminine voice cut into his reverie. Quickly, Peter put Griffin's letter away before it could attract notice. Then he carefully fixed his expression and slowly turned around to greet the bearer of the voice. She was one of the many acquaintances he had made since coming west to Hollywood, an actress of exceptional skill.

Lily Cahill was a tigress. The actress's uncommon beauty coupled with her steely predatory nature, earned her the nickname on the lot of

"Tiger Lily," a fusion of both flower and beast. Her reputation was that of a man-eater, and currently, it was Peter she wanted to devour.

From their initial introduction on the set, Peter could not help but sense that the Tiger Lily wanted to be something to him. Cold and amorous by turns, she was accustomed to getting whatever she set her sights on. Unfortunately for Peter, once she fixed her sites on him, his polite attempts at distance did little to hinder her purpose.

Already leading lady onscreen to Peter's leading man, for reasons he could not begin to fathom, she was equally determined to assume the role in real life. Since they were working together and he could not hope to avoid her, Peter decided to make the best of the situation and befriend the wayward beauty.

Patiently, he waited while Lily tottered after him. "Peter, darling," she growled, catching up and securing herself to him by entangling her arm through his. "D.W. has invited us to dinner this Saturday. Lionel and Doris will be there, as will Harry, Elmer, Mary, and of course, Dorothy and Lillian." She nearly purred with excitement. "You've never seen D.W.'s house on Prospect Avenue, have you?"

Peter shook his head, knowing that was all that was required to keep up his end of the conversation. She continued, her violet eyes blazing with triumph, "It's a grand house. Someday we'll have a house as fine—finer—the finest house on Prospect Avenue, and it will be a great honor to dine with *us*."

Peter crooked an eyebrow, but Lily was too far into her schemes to notice. She'd been doing that more and more—using "us" and "we" as if their relationship was inevitable and mutual. If she persisted, he was going to have to think seriously about returning to the New York stage. Idly, he wondered if the Bishop would renew his offer of patronage.

Accustomed to tuning Lily out and pursuing his own train of

thought, Peter registered her current topic with some delay, as if from a great distance...

She had been babbling on about an engagement party and her surprise at their being D.W.'s guests of honor. Suddenly, he wasn't following. It was as if he was missing a critical piece of information. Then he had a sinking feeling in his stomach of the most acute variety.

"Wait," he sputtered. "This dinner at D.W.'s is to be an engagement party?"

"Yes," Lily purred, her French-manicured fingertips smoothing an errant, dark curl from her eyes. "Isn't that fabulous of him? I haven't the slightest idea what I'm going to wear."

The world slowed to a dead stop, and Peter with it. "I haven't heard of any recent engagement." The final word caught in his throat, and he tried to clear the thick dread that had settled there with it.

"Haven't you?" Lily asked nonchalantly, unable to meet his glare. "It was on the front page of today's society column." She laughed nervously. "That must be how D.W. found out."

Peter felt numb. "Found out about whom?"

Hedging, Lily ran her fingers lightly up and down his forearm, chiding, "You really ought to read the society column, you know."

"Who?" The question was flat but not emotionless.

Lily raised her hand to her throat as if offended. "Why *us*, silly."

The world, already stopped, tinted red and Peter understood for the first time what it was to be in a murderous rage. His hands fisted reflexively as ice-cold anger flowed through his veins. He took a deep breath, dragging air through his clenched teeth in an attempt to calm himself. He couldn't look at her. "Why would they think that?"

Her eyes widened in shock as Peter disentangled himself. "You don't believe *I* had anything to do with this, do you? I thought that you were behind it." She looked confused, then vulnerable. Her violet eyes sparkled with unshed tears as she admitted haltingly, "I thought you wanted to surprise me—that you had—finally—that you—felt—the same way—I do."

Peter knew she was just talented enough not to be believed. Still remote, he said in a low voice, "I want it retracted."

Changing tactics, the tigress grabbed at his arm. "Just think about this for a moment. It's great publicity for the picture. 'Lily Cahill and Peter Neverland—sweethearts on and off the silver screen.' We *will* be America's sweethearts."

Clinging to his control, to keep the growing impulse to do violence at bay, he managed one word. "No!"

She stepped in front of him, turning to face him with her hands flat against his chest. "Don't be hasty, Peter. In addition to the publicity, there are other benefits to being engaged. Benefits that even you cannot object to." She drew her palms slowly down the length of his chest, toying playfully with the waistband of his trousers and Peter's traitorous body responded in spite of his resolve. Triumphant, she set her jaw, daring him to negate her.

His anger melted away as he considered her proposal with revulsion. Maybe his broken heart did not mean he could not partake in convenient companionship...but he had to be honest with Lily. Although young, he would never be the sort of man to confuse lust with love. "I will never love you," he stated matter-of-factly.

Lily raised her eyebrows and let out a harsh laugh that sounded more like a bray. "Silly boy, since when do engagements have anything to do with love?"

The woman in front of him suddenly seemed worldly, experienced, and tarnished from use. Peter felt as if a veil had been lifted and he was seeing her for the first time. What he saw scared him. He had sorely underestimated the Tiger Lily and for that mistake, she had devoured him whole.

Avast belay, yo ho...

Of late, Peter's dreams had been heavier—not the chaotic whirling scenes he was accustomed to—but something nefariously darker and cumbersome. Blackness, thick and still, then the faintest taste of malice in the air, a whisper of violence in the wind... Something was blowing his way, wicked and unstoppable. In the distance he could hear Indians on the warpath, and tight on their heels, a steady ticking. But what was troubling him was closer. There on the breeze, the faintest hint of a diabolical song—

Avast belay, yo ho, A-pirating we go...

It was the sound of evil, carousing and hungry. The sound of pirates on the prowl.

12

The Return Home

"Engaged?" Wendy felt the color drain from her face, her teacup suspended in mid-air, forgotten.

"I am afraid so, dearest." Maimie bit her bottom lip in concern, watching her friend for signs of a relapse into melancholia. "I didn't want you to hear it in the street. Was I right to tell you?" Wendy remained frozen for so long that Maimie opened her mouth to repeat the question.

"Yes," Wendy said hastily, managing a wan smile before taking a long sip from her cup. "It helps me greatly to know he has moved on…as have I."

Maimie narrowed her eyes, unconvinced. "Hmm."

"Truly," Wendy managed with more animation. To underscore the point, she helped herself to a biscuit.

She returned from her uneventful tea to find James pacing in the garden. There was a nervous purpose in his movements as the young banker silently presented her with a handpicked bouquet of flowers. Ignoring the questioning look on her face, he clasped her hand and led her to a nearby bench.

As soon as she sat, Wendy leapt back up. Unable to remain still, she took over pacing, her force and momentum driving her forward. She felt reckless—like a woman with nothing left to lose and quickly shut the thought down. *Actually,* she lied to herself, *it would be a relief to consign myself to fate.*

James watched her without speaking. She had no idea what was going on in his taciturn mind and doubted she ever would. They had no particular connection in that way. After all, he was not Peter. No. James was dull and boring, and patient and loyal. Peter, for all his passion, had been nothing but the source of unmitigated heartbreak. Peter had abandoned her for another county, another girl. In truth, he had never actually claimed Wendy for his own, but he had undoubtedly felt that same earth shattering connection as she. Hadn't he?

Everything deflated in that moment, as Wendy acknowledged that Peter most likely existed in blissful ignorance of her affections toward him. She was nothing to him, save the import she had created in her own mind. Suddenly she felt chilled. Pulling her shawl tighter about her shoulders, she slowly crossed the garden to sit next to James. "Perhaps," she began dully, "we should stop hedging around the future and reach an agreement."

Quietly, James nodded. Then he dropped to his knee to ask *the* question that was a death sentence to her spirit.

The boy came to her again that night. From the open window, he beckoned her. "Wendy, Wendy," he called. "When you are sleeping in your bed you might be flying about with me saying funny things to the stars." She liked the sound of that, flying with the boy, leaving her nightmares and troubles behind.

With growing excitement Wendy approached the window and the boy's outstretched hand. But as she reached for him, the boy saw something on her face that caused him to gasp. Hastily, he pulled his hand away as if too close to an open flame.

"Wendy," he accused, "you've given my place to another! Soon someone will share your bed, and I shan't be able to see you anymore."

"No," she contradicted, "I haven't replaced you. You may always return."

But the boy clamped his hands over his ears, squeezed his eyes shut and bemoaned, "Nay, what have you done Wendy? What have you done?"

Lily certainly had her finer points, Peter reflected as he watched her work D.W. Griffith's parlor. In addition to her consummate publicity skills, she was stunning to look at and good company, when she wasn't playing at being coquettish.

He supposed there were worse things than being engaged to such a desirable woman. She might even make a decent wife—for someone—just not him. Not that he hadn't tried to find some measure of feeling for her. He had dug deep within himself, but the most he could coax from the shriveled up organ that had once been his heart was sisterly affection.

Despite his lack of attachment, it was his tenuous honor that kept him from acting on Lily's suggestion that they become more than friends toward one another. From his end, their engagement was a practical business arrangement, and despite her blatant offers to make it more, Peter could not take advantage.

Usually that was the end of that line of thought, but tonight, watching the ravishing Tiger Lily weave her magic spell on those around her, he was tempted to put his honor aside. Surely he had enough flaws in his character to accomplish what every other man in the room was clearly fantasizing about? She was, after all, his fiancée.

But where his honor might have failed him, the matter of her honor kept him steadfast. It was not right to treat a woman such—even if the woman asked for it.

With a reluctant sigh, Peter helped himself to another glass of D .W.'s finest Scotch and retreated to the quiet sanctuary of his host's well-stocked library. Without conscious thought, he selected a slim volume of Shakespeare's sonnets. Absently fingering the exquisite binding, he seated himself opposite the roaring fire, deep in thought.

"Thinking on matters of the heart, lad?"

The deep resonate voice startled him, for he thought himself alone in his reverie. It did not surprise him that his host had sought out solitude as well. D.W. often stole away when in the grips of artistic contemplation.

Peter noted with irony the book he had selected at random. "Am I that transparent?"

"To most no, but to me..." D.W. smiled enigmatically, nodding at the book Peter held in his hands. His host raised his amber-filled tumbler in salute and took a hearty drink.

Peter respected the opinion of the director and head of Biograph films. He was an authoritative man, like a shrewd general, but also a forward-thinking visionary. Peter found himself curious of the good man's opinion. "And just what is amiss, do you think?"

"Passion," he replied without hesitation. "Not that you lack passion, my lad—you have it in spades for the camera. But in your real life, you and Lily do not mesh—no matter how hard she tries to force it."

"Aye," Peter agreed draining his own Scotch. "She does try." He half expected the older man's candidness to unnerve him but, instead, found it refreshing. He realized he enjoyed being exposed and the rare honesty it afforded him. "I keep thinking if I try hard enough, I can learn to love her."

D.W. let out a surprised grunt. Decanting a nearly empty bottle of booze, he refilled his glass before passing the bottle to Peter. "You can teach the mind to do many things, my lad, but the heart... Well the heart is another matter entirely."

"And what if you have no heart?"

The director scrutinized him for few moments before answering. "You most certainly have a heart, lad. So tell me, where have you left it?"

Considering with whom he conversed, the question shouldn't have surprised him, but it unsettled him nonetheless. He swallowed half his drink before acquiescing with a sigh. "Across the ocean—a long time ago."

"Perhaps you should go in search of it."

Peter sighed, embracing the veracity of the moment. "As much as I dream to the contrary, the lady cares nothing for me."

D.W. nodded sagely. "I wondered if your most recent letter from abroad contained bad tidings. I somehow sensed it might."

Peter started. "Which letter?"

"The one that arrived last Wednesday," Peter's uncomprehending expression caused the other man to continue carefully. "It arrived after our last shoot... You had gone for the day... I gave it to Lily to give to you... When I asked her the next day, she confirmed that she had..." The look on Peter's face caused the director to falter. "She kept if from you then?"

Shaking his head back and forth, Peter said in a low voice, "I haven't received a letter from home in nearly three months." With a hard set to his jaw, Peter rose. "Excuse me please. I believe I need to have a word with my *fiancée*."

Leaping to his feet, D.W. caught Peter's arm. "Allow me, my lad. Perhaps it would be more prudent if I sent your fiancée to you." Peter could only nod dumbly at the suggestion. He appreciated the discretion but lacked the ability to voice the words.

After D.W.'s departure, Peter emptied the bottle into his glass, but rather than finish the contents, he crossed stiffly to the mantle, deliberately placing his back to the door. The fire seemed to mirror the rage churning inside of him. Why would Lily keep correspondence from him? Didn't she understand he was a man dying of thirst and it was only those letters that kept him alive? He could go for months on the sustenance that one sentence about *her* provided. Knowing *she* lived, despite the pain caused by the details, made it possible to go on. How could Lily rob him of his only nourishment–indeed of his very life?

Two distinct pairs of footsteps echoed behind him, and he grasped for control, knowing he teetered on the edge of a precipice.

Lily crossed to him and hugged him from behind. "There you are, my darling. I daresay that everyone has been looking for your charming self."

Peter felt cold to his core. He dared not move, lest his wrath get the better of him. With calm he did not feel, he stated, "I believe you have something of mine."

"I can't think what, darling." Lily placed a kiss against his neck, causing him to stiffen ever so slightly.

From the doorway, D.W. clear his throat. "Perhaps I should be seeing to my guests." He asked Peter pointedly, "Shall I go, lad?"

"No." Peter wrenched himself out of Lily's arms and took a deep, calming breath, before turning around. "I mean, please stay D.W., since this concerns you." His fierce scowl turned on Lily who pretended to smile bravely in the face of it. "Tell me Lily, did D.W. recently give you anything to give to me? A letter maybe?"

She looked from one man to the other and found nothing encouraging in either countenance. Pretending to think hard on it, she remembered slowly. "Now that you mention it, I did have a letter to give to you." She let out a brief musical laugh. "It must have slipped my mind, until this very moment. Sorry."

"Damn your sorry," Peter growled. "I want that letter. Now!"

"Of course, Peter." Lily was a composition of innocence. "I would have given it to you sooner, if I hadn't truly forgotten."

She rummaged about in her handbag and pulled out a familiar cream envelope. Peter snatched it from her hand, anxiously noting the London post mark before turning it over. Then he stopped dead in his tracks. "It's been opened," he stated flatly.

"It came like tha—"

"Get out!" Peter rarely got angry, so to hear him bellow, see him quaking with rage, was a fearsome sight indeed. Blanching, Lily wisely closed her mouth and let D.W. lead her from the room. Peter had no presence of mind to take note of their leaving. He was singularly focused on the letter and his wild thoughts about the tidings it contained. Chilled to the bone, he reseated himself in front of the fire and drained his scotch in one greedy gulp. Then with trembling hands, he opened his most recent letter from his brother.

Inside was the expected single page of matching stationary filled with Griffin's sturdy script. Unexpected were the two newspaper clippings that fluttered quietly onto Peter's lap.

Which to read first?

Peter sat for a long time unable to read anything. At length, he made up his mind to start with the letter, lest the clippings contained notices that might be taken out of context. Wishing he had another tumbler of Scotch to fortify himself, he eased the letter open and willed himself to read the first words.

Dearest Brother, Griffin's greeting was usually a balm to his soul, but not today. *First I want to offer my congratulations! Though I am quite put out that I had to learn of your good tidings from London's society column rather than your own hand. Please let me know when the blessed event will occur so that I can make the proper travel arrangements. It is of no use to dissuade me, for there is no distance I would not traverse to partake in your happiness. It does my heart glad to think you have finally found respite from your agony!*

In light of such gladsome tidings, I hope I am not amiss in including another bit of news from London's society pages. Perhaps now that you have found your own joy, it will give you the closure you so desperately need.

I remain as always, you loving brother.

Griffin.

Despite the fire, Peter shivered. His stomach churned unpleasantly, and he could not seem to find his breath. In the corner of his eye, he noticed that D.W. had returned but remained prudently in the doorway. With growing dread, he picked up the two newspaper clippings that had accompanied Griffin's tidings. Willing his eyes to focus, he scanned the first one. It was a recent account of his engagement to Lily published in the London Herald. *Damn!* It had never occurred to him this bit of folly would be noteworthy enough to become news back home.

Cursing under his breath, he hastily examined the other paper. It was another engagement notice. This one however, announced the upcoming nuptials of one James Christopher Whitby III to one Wendy Moira Angela Darling.

The words, in black and white print, seemed to have no initial effect on him. In a stupor, he stood with the intent of finding more scotch. Peter had taken a mere handful of steps before his heart pitched sharply against his chest and he doubled over uttering a hollow groan.

"Let me help you, lad."

Peter heard D.W. coming to his assistance, felt the good man reach out to support his arm but found himself impervious to his host's kindness. Through clenched teeth, he spoke. "I'm all right!"

"But, my lad, you're in pain."

He shook out of the man's fatherly grasp. "It isn't that kind of pain," Peter replied darkly. His strength failed him, and he sunk to his knees, while the two announcements mingled in his brain. Scanning the clippings for confirmation, he marked that Wendy's notice was exactly one week after his own appeared. Was the timing a coincidence? He didn't dare think otherwise—that his notice would have in any way influenced Wendy's decision. *Impossible!*

And yet deep inside, the innocent part of Peter—that part which refused to grow up and harden into a man—pleaded with him for adherence. First a quiet whisper, growing louder and more sure, then into a deafening roar, a cacophony.

'Tis true, the childish voice inside him cried, *she was driven to such measures by you Peter!* He shook his head to clear it, but the voice would not be silenced. *'Tis true Peter. By you...*

Abruptly Peter straightened, his purpose startlingly clear before him. He laid an apologetic hand on D.W. Griffith's arm. "I'm sorry, Sir. I must away."

"Of course," nodded the other sympathetically. "I dare say things will seem better tomorrow."

"I shan't be here on the morrow." Peter said the last over his shoulder, as he was striding toward the door.

Comprehension must have sunk in because D.W. called after him in alarm, "Just where are you going, lad?"

"Home," Peter said surely. "To reclaim my heart."

The following night as Peter slept in his drawing room aboard a train bound for New York, he dreamt of his return home. *Impatient, he had forsaken modern modes of travel and simply flown the distance. Up ahead was London, deep in slumber and lit by a backdrop of twinkling stars. And look, there was Wendy's street! Although he had been away for moons and moons and moons, he knew she would always keep the window open for him.*

Look, up ahead—No. 14, and there, Wendy's window; but as he came upon the house, the window was barred. Wendy had forgotten about him, and another pale head was in her bed, sleeping aside her where Peter ought to have been.

His agony was exquisite as he grasped the bars, staring at the scene within. Peter realized then that he was looking through the window at the one joy from which he must be forever barred.

13

Wendy Grows Up

Something as dark as night had come into Wendy's life...

Though it was a glorious sun-drenched morning and she was soaking in a hot bath, Wendy could not rid herself of the chill that crept up her spine. Distractedly, she watched ripples work their way across the water's surface like little shivers. Her recent dreams, almost always centering on the ocean or a ship, were increasing in violence and incomprehension. There were men, a most villainous-looking lot of pirates, intent on doing her harm. Without benefit of words, she felt their black intensions.

Their dreadful song still echoed in her ears.

Yo ho, yo ho, the frisky plank,

You walks along it so,

Till it goes down and you goes down

To Davy Jones below!

She oft dreamt of pirates in her life, but lately, there was none of the thrilling adventure and thrice the terror. Her dread of them, both asleep and awake, was suffocating. These were no ordinary dreams, but nightmares that clung to her person upon waking like a putrid sludge. Each night upon closing her eyes, their malice drew closer and Wendy prayed for the return of one person who could save her from their horrible fate. But Peter remained heartlessly absent. Leaving her at their awful mercy, alone and utterly unprotected.

Running her hands across her temples, Wendy sought to push the dreams out of her head. She ascribed them to being a newly engaged woman. It was normal to have doubts before the wedding, even of the most fatalistic kind. Both her mother and Aunt Mildred had judiciously told her so, although how her spinster Aunt would know about such things was beyond Wendy's comprehension.

Ringing for old Liza, Wendy began to dress for the engagement dinner her future in-laws were hosting in hers and James's honor. It was of great relief that Viscount Withington and Maimie were on the guest list. How Wendy had missed her dear friend these past months. Maimie's pregnancy confinement had taken its toll on the both of them. Now that she had delivered the Viscount a healthy heir, she was again free, and the Viscount again neglectfully aloof.

Maimie had taken well to motherhood. Of course, it was easy to mother when you had someone else to bathe, feed and change your bundle of joy. Still, at times, Wendy couldn't help but wonder if her friend's glow was as much motherhood as the fact that since achieving progeny the Viscount had taken to a separate bedchamber.

Wendy was still young and inexperienced enough in the ways of the world to feel sure that her marriage would be different. Not a marriage of convenience, but one of partnership and a shared bed, no matter how many offspring were produced. To wish for a marriage based in passionate love might be overreaching—she was no longer that foolishly young—but mutual fondness and genuine caring seemed a goodly lot to achieve in such a callous world.

The Whitby's lived on Park Lane, in a modern edifice of stone and glass just round the corner from Apsley House. They were one of those grand families that everyone generally admired but no one thought particularly much of. They were pleasant, if bland, and accepting, within certain circles. Already they had embraced Wendy as a most-beloved daughter, although the type of daughter they thought her to be remained most unclear.

As the car pulled into the pristine half-moon drive and James stood gravely by, waiting, Wendy was grateful that she had the foresight to send her family on ahead. During their last outing, James had intimated he wanted to speak to her alone, although what he could possibly need to say that could not be discussed in front of their friends, Wendy could scarcely imagine.

Agreeing to a turn in the garden, they walked in silence for some moments before James got to the point of his request. "Miss Darling—"

"James, we are to be married soon. At some point, you must learn to use my Christian name." Her eyes twinkled in amusement at her betrothed's obvious discomfort. "Wendy."

"Right," James drew in a deep breath before starting again with chagrin. "Miss—her—I mean, Wendy. I may not be a shrewd man, but I am not so dense as to fail to notice that I care a great deal more for you than you do for me."

The statement, although apt, offended Wendy deeply. It was the kind of truth that, if overheard, would make others think poorly of the both of them. "Nonsense James—"

Cutting off her protestations with an upturned hand, James continued. "I am not a fool, Wendy. I realize you do not love me. And I know that you are feeling pressured as much as I to enter into a favorable match.

The difference between our situations is that I genuinely feel for you, and I had hoped with time you would care the same way about me."

Hearing her private thoughts spoken so sensibly from James caused Wendy's cheeks to burn with humiliation. Unable to form words of protest, she stared at him open mouthed. Even if she had known what to say to negate him, would she dare indulge in such bold-face lies?

Pacing away from Wendy, James directed his wistfulness at a small tree erupting with tiny pink buds. "You see, I want a proper home...and children, and laughter... I can live without love, if you can give me those things. If you can respect me and learn to care for me, I will be content. But if I am asking too much, or if you have committed your heart elsewhere, then I release you."

Wendy started to attest that she had accepted his engagement and was therefore committed to him, when he annoyingly cut her off again. "Do not speak now, and please know that I will not think ill of you, no matter what you choose. If you are ready to embrace a life with me, then come to the house to celebrate. If you are not able to do as I ask...then go from this place with my blessing and my most fervent wish for a long and happy life."

Watching James's retreating form, Wendy took a strange pride in his resolute carriage which conveyed both sides of his firm yet gentle nature. He would make a great husband—for some lucky woman—but...was that woman to be her?

James, as usual, was the voice of all things logical. For a family and the blessings of motherhood, one could forsake passion. It was a wise, practical and very grown-up decision. Isn't that what her own mother and Maimie—indeed most women—did?

Taking a deep breath, she knew she had mere minutes to decide the matter before her mother, or worse Aunt Mildred, came in search of her. How James had guessed at her otherwise engaged affections she could not tell, but he had released her to follow her heart. Had she not already tried that with disastrous results, she might be sorely tempted now. However, the debacle of trying to catch Peter's ship had put her in bed for weeks with heartbreak. And while Maimie would still urge her to follow a certain actor to America, she was not hearty enough to leave everything behind on a whim and the vague hope of requited love.

No, when it came to impetuousness, Wendy was weak. But she was loyal and true, and when she loved, she loved with her whole heart. It occurred to her then that her fault was not a lack of bravery to act, but that she loved so in the first place. It was such a delightfully mature thought that when something deep inside of her rebelled obstinately at the folly of her logic, Wendy refused to pay any heed.

Noise, the rustling of skirts coming down the garden walk caused her to steel herself. But instead of Aunt Mildred's severe glare, it was her dearest friend's compassionate face that came presently into view.

"There you are, dearest." Maimie said, her delight at encountering her friend lighting up her pretty features. "Your Aunt Mildred is in quite rare form. From the way she's carrying on to the Whitbys, you'd think she was to marry James instead of you."

Wendy had never been as happy in her whole life to see her sympathetic, true friend. When Maimie had rounded the bend, the relief that coursed through Wendy's body had been instantaneous and all-encompassing. Not only would she have a few more minutes to make the most important decision of her life, but she now had near her the one person whose very presence was a comfort to her soul. Although Maimie had made her thoughts and feelings on Peter Neverland quite clear, she'd said very little of late about Wendy's intended.

"Maimie," Wendy began uncertainly, "you do *like* James, do you not?"

"Of course." Maimie's smile was genuine, without malice or mockery.

"And have you always liked him or...have you learned to like him, since we... I mean, since I..."

...settled for him?"

Bristling at having the truth spoken so bluntly for the second time in the same hour, she protested, "I have not settled!"

"You have—and it's fine, Dearest. I liked James before all that. Just so happens that I liked someone else for you better."

"Why?" Wendy looked down at the gray, pebble-strewn path, afraid if she met Maimie's astute gaze, the girl would read her too clearly. "I mean, why Peter?"

"Because you're in love with him. You have been, from the moment you laid eyes on him, and I am convinced you always shall be."

"How do you know?"

"I've never been in love myself, but I've seen it. On stage and in real life. When you have a marriage such as mine, it is impossible not to recognize the genuine thing when it crosses your path. The kind of love that makes one do the most foolish and nonsensical things—like chasing ships and crossing oceans. The kind of love that makes one's heart take wing to defy the laws of nature and man." Maimie paused, and Wendy made the mistake of looking up into her friend's impassioned face. "The kind of love you hold for Peter."

"But," Wendy argued, "if that love, no matter how strong, is completely one-sided, is it not in fact, something else altogether? Something unhealthy?"

Maimie dismissed her reasoning with a small huff. "Until you hear Peter's feeling from his own mouth, I would not deign to make such presumptions. There's still time to follow him to—"

"No." Shaking her head back and forth, Wendy tried to dispel the odious memory of her frantic behavior on the jetty as Peter's ship had sailed away. Never before or hence had she felt so helpless or alone. With James, she had certainly never experienced the relentless myriad of unsettling emotions that every encounter or thought of Peter seemed to produce. In fact, with James she felt quite the opposite, secure and stable—no amazing highs but more importantly no devastating lows.

Suddenly, Wendy realized her choice was already made. "No," she repeated, "my family and my life are here. There's no reason why I shouldn't be reasonably content with James. And above all, I have you. Will you help me?"

Despite the tears shining like jewels in her eyes, Maimie nodded. "Anything, Dearest."

"Help me to pretend that Peter never existed and that James is my first choice."

"If that's truly what you want—"

"It is."

"Then yes." The girl linked her arm through Wendy's in a display of sisterly camaraderie. "We shall both delude ourselves to be madly in love, together."

As they walked toward the Whitby house arm in arm, Wendy couldn't help feeling she had navigated a fork in the road and, after committing to a direction, had once again chosen the safe, sensible path.

No, she was not strong like Maimie, but Wendy could be strong in her own way. She would embrace that which life had offered to her, companionship and mutual caring. And above all friendship. And despite today signifying the end of her girlhood dreams, Wendy was strong enough to accept her life-to-be as Mrs. James Christopher Whitby III with a measure of gladness.

Shoulders back, head high, Wendy resolutely followed the winding path that would lead her out of the garden of temptations into her chosen life. As she walked, she smiled in earnest, feeling for the first time like a woman in control of her own destiny.

A fortnight after leaving Hollywood behind, Peter stood on the deck of the mighty sea vessel the *Lusitania*, contemplating the darkness. Since the debacle in the dining room the first night aboard ship of trying to make polite conversation amidst his total distraction, Peter had shunned the other passengers, preferring instead to take his meals in his rooms.

How different was this crossing than the previous one with Mr. Frohman and Mr. Boucicault. Then, he had the whole world in front of him to experience and the vague inclination he could outdistance his memories. Ironically, in all those months in America those memories had remained his most faithful companions.

He was anxious to be home and yet scared of what would happen once he arrived. His own skin felt alien, as if he had been cast into a fictional story. Every moment, he feared was about to be his last as his imagination conjured up every manner of disaster from rogue waves, to crocodiles and pirates. Interruptions he both dreaded and longed for.

Often he'd reflected on the poor, unfortunate girl from the jetty, the one who'd caught Mr. Boucicault's fancy enough to remark upon. Although Peter had not witnessed her for himself, he oft imagined she was a ghost. Since the start of this voyage, to Peter's mind she'd become an apparition of Wendy's spirit beseeching him not to leave her.

Peter attributed his illogical fancies and the growing unease they produced to guilt. He felt terrible about letting D.W. and the rest of the Biograph Company down. They would have to recast and reshoot all Peter's scenes, a fact the Tiger Lily was none too pleased with. Peter remained tormented by their final—and very confusing—confrontation.

Despite the certainty Peter felt that Lily would recast him off-screen, the actress seemed loath to let her leading man go. She had followed him from D.W.'s party to his rooms, barging in on him as he haphazardly packed his belongings, his head spinning slightly from Scotch and revelation.

"Peter darling," she had purred as if all was right between them. "Whatever are you doing?"

"Returning to England."

"You cannot be serious. Because of our tiff?" She pouted her lower lip and batted her eyelashes at him then. "Would it amend things if I said I was sorry? Because I am, Love."

Peter stiffened giving her the merest of fleeting glances. "Don't call me that." Turning back to his chore, he focused on the task, deciding to ignore Lily until he could walk out the door and away from her for good.

"Call you what? Love? Don't you deserve love Peter?" She let the question lie between them for some time before continuing in a husky voice. "Don't you want love?" In the pause, Lily had shimmied out of her gown and was now approaching him clad only in her slip.

Shocked by her brazenness, Peter stared as the Tiger Lily moved in for the kill. She put his hands on her hips as she leaned close, whispering, "Don't you want me? I can show you love."

"No."

"Your mouth says, 'No' but your body is saying, 'Yes!'"

Pressing her lips against his neck she repeated, "Yes!" Then they were kissing, the kind of kisses that are full of liquor and violence and can never amount to anything satisfying.

Lily backed him across the room until the backs of his knees bumped the bed and they fell into a tangled heap. "Say you will stay," she commanded, pulling at his hair.

"No." Despite his answer, he did not pull away.

"Then take me with you," she hissed.

In the end, it was Lily's own words evoking thoughts of home and of Wendy that saved him. Pain returned—an excruciating mass in his chest—at the thought of his beloved in another's arms.

Feeling the weight of betrayal, he roughly pulled back from Lily's claws and, gathering up what he could, walked away without so much as a goodbye. Enraged, Lily shouted at his back, "Whoever your little harlot is, she'll never love you!"

Her parting words hit their mark, filling Peter with uncertainty for the future but leaving no doubts about his decision to go. No. What he had left behind in the West would not be missed.

Unconsciously, he slipped his talisman, the little thimble half, from his pocket and soothed himself by tracing its contours. Returning home was an errand of folly and although he had moments of purpose and certainly, he was assailed by doubts. He had no assurances to believe upon his return that he would be embraced rather than smacked. But he couldn't not go. Couldn't not try...

He should not, indeed had no right to, feel the way he did about Wendy's engagement. She did not belong to him—quite the opposite. And yet, it was as if she were some vital organ, without which he would certainly perish.

Returning the talisman to his pocket, his fingers brushed against the many pages of parchment resting within. The half-written letters were all poor attempts to announce his imminent arrival to Griffin and all abandoned for lack of a sane explanation. What could he say? He was returning to England to incur one last foolish encounter with the love of his life before she pledged herself to another? Or perhaps that he was coming to foil Wendy's marriage by professing his love? No matter the reason, when written down it sounded flimsy and full of vain conceit.

There was that part of Peter, the sensible part, who wanted to turn around and do his best to get on with his new life in America. But there was also the hopeless romantic part, who believed his grand gesture would sweep Wendy Moira Angela Darling off her feet. Beyond that was the greater part of Peter, who could not in good conscious give up without a fight. No matter how immature and boyish, he had not done right by that part of himself.

Back to London he would go then, to fight for Wendy's hand. Hopefully, he would not damage his propriety or irrevocably injure his romantic side in the process. But the closer he got to home, and Wendy, the more oppressive his doubt became.

This doubt produced the most terrifying dreams. The one that had woken him not an hour earlier had been the worst yet. Bracing himself with a lungful of salty, sea air, he forced himself to reexamine the details.

Wendy adrift...

The waves were tossing her, taking her out to sea. Peter's lungs ached and his arms cramped with exertion. With a final lunge, he grasped her hand and began swimming toward the closest rock. With herculean effort, he hoisted Wendy into a small crevasse and pulled himself up to rest beside her. She was cold and trembling but alive. Wrapping a protective arm about her waist, Peter passed out.

Time stopped until he was aware of something slipping from his grasp. Blinking his eyes, he wildly looked around trying to put the scene into context. A ways off, he saw a brief shimmer of gold deep below the water's surface, then the image was obscured by the flip of pearlescent green scales. A mermaid's tail.

Suddenly Peter realized that he was alone on the rock. Sick with dread he looked for the shimmer of gold, beneath the water's surface but it was gone. With horror, Peter realized that he had let Wendy go— he had let her drown.

He had woken himself up, crying out, "I'm sorry, Wendy! I'm sorry!"

Now standing stoically sentinel at the bow, facing eastward as the ship sliced through the Atlantic Ocean, he did his best to let the nightmare go. Propelled forward by steel and sheer determination, he could almost believe himself to be the valiant underdog backed by fate; as if the ship and everyone on it were conspiring to his purpose.

It was such flashes of optimism he now lived for. If only he could hold on to those lovely wonderful thoughts, harness their power to make the ship go faster, or better yet lift the ship up into the air. What time it would save if the ship could take flight.

Crumpling up the half-written letter into a paper ball, he hurled it into the ocean. Then he lifted his ever-present talisman reverently to his lips. Shutting his eyes, he made a wish on the second star to his right. *Please*, he beseeched the heavens, *please work your will.* In that moment the strangest of sensations settled over him and Peter felt the urge to crow.

14

The Boy in the Theatre

*A*t some point on the journey from Wales to London the gentle rocking of the train shifted into a choppy turbulence as Peter flew through the darkened skies with a singular purpose. But what purpose?

Look! Ahead in the mist—a flash of the Jolly Roger; the tip of a wooden plank. And above, the chaotic billowing of a night dress. Wendy!

She was bound, and on the pirate ship; she who loved everything to be just so! As the plank receded Peter focused all his speed into interrupting her fall. "I'll save her!" he cried.

The instant Peter arrived in London he set off on an errand of the greatest urgency. Being Saturday afternoon, he headed straightaway for his former haven, The Duke of York's Theatre. If he hurried, he would just make the final curtain. Although he had missed the place, it was not the theatre that drew him; it was the hope of encountering the faithful patroness who attended every matinee from the dress circle.

Peter sought Wendy, but in all actuality, it felt as if he were seeking his very self. How fortunate his arrival in the familiar lobby coincided with the exit of the matinee audience. Careful to keep to the shadows, Peter prowled the perimeter of the crowd, searching for his love.

"How romantic it was. Do you not agree Miss Darling?"

On hearing Wendy's name, Peter spun around nearly colliding with a mass of blonde curls. The respondent, who kept her back to him, inclined her head in genteel agreement.

"Indeed."

Peter inched closer to better overhear their conversation.

"The romance was extraordinary. It reminded me so very much of your courtship to my cousin James. How happy he has made you and how very much you worship him. Isn't that right Miss Darling?"

In most enthusiastic tones, Wendy answered, "Exactly so, Miss Geoghegan."

What a narcissistic creature Peter was! This was the first time since his decision to return that Peter stopped to consider the prospect of Wendy's happiness. Not only did her intended make her happy, she *worshipped* him. Unable to help himself, he repositioned himself to better observe Wendy's profile as her companion continued to talk.

"I knew it, Miss Darling. I have a sense about these things. If there's anything I am an expert in, it is evidence of true love."

"I dare say you are spot on." Wendy's agreeable smile was heartbreaking in its sweetness. It might as well have been a cannonball for the pain it inflicted on him.

"This was lovely," the companion declared. "We should do this again, Miss Darling. Soon and often."

If I cannot be with her, Peter thought dejectedly, *I can at least hope to remain close to her each week at the matinee. Perhaps I can be content to stand near and love her from afar...*

The last shred of hope to which Peter could cling was ripped from his hands with Wendy Darling's emphatic reply. "In truth, Miss Geoghegan, I expect to be so divinely happy in marital bliss that I shan't have any further use for the theatre and its world of make believe."

Turning on his heels, Peter retreated leaving his shattered hopes on the floor of the lobby amidst the discarded programmes.

"How romantic it was. Do you not agree Miss Darling?"

Wendy inclined her head in genteel, if noncommittal, agreement. "Indeed."

She was not fond of James's visiting cousin, Winifred "Winnie" Geoghegan. Winnie was a silly sort of girl whose head swam with ridiculous notions of romantic love but lacked the sensibility to temper those thoughts with any practicality. In addition to her preposterous notions of courtship, she was an accomplished talker, which in Wendy's good opinion should never be mistaken for conversation. With the slightest encouragement, Winnie could prattle on for hours concerning subjects of the littlest import.

How she missed dear Maimie. Unfortunately, Maimie's mother was not well at present, and it was a daughter's duty to attend to the person responsible for her birth. It was Aunt Mildred who had suggested Winnie would make a suitable substitute for her truest companion. Like most things concerning Wendy's life, Aunt Mildred had been sorely mistaken.

Winnie was a dreadful stand-in. Incapable of remaining quiet, she punctuated the play with a steady stream of whispered commentary.

Even though Wendy refused to reply, the girl did not shut up. Wendy couldn't ever remember a matinee as odious as this afternoon spent with Winnie.

"Isn't that right Miss Darling?"

Drat! She had been saying something—terribly dull no doubt—about the play. With an enthusiastic smile, Wendy answered, "Exactly so, Miss Geoghegan."

Winnie grinned, losing her thin lips in the process. "I knew it, Miss Darling. I have a sense about these things. If there's anything I am an expert in, it is the evidence of true love."

Still having no idea what the original topic had been, Wendy ventured, "I dare say you are spot on."

If only she had turned around, Wendy would have not failed to notice the achingly familiar young man, with the piercing emerald eyes, eavesdropping. She would have marked the devastated expression of the young actor whose hopes and dreams were—at that very moment—being dashed to pieces, and perhaps given pause to her improvised replies. But she remained hopelessly ignorant, her attention focused on discovering the topic of her current discourse.

"This was lovely. We should do this again, Miss Darling. Soon and often."

The prospect of more disagreeable outings with Winnie—soon and often—caused Wendy to utter the first excuse she could think of. It was, unfortunately, an outrageous lie. "In truth, Miss Geoghegan, I expect to be so divinely happy in marital bliss that I shall have no further use for the theatre and its world of make believe."

At the time, Wendy felt pride regarding her artful evasion. If only she had realized the smallness of her world, where even the most intimate of conversations fell on outside ears and every lie had its consequence...

The dream was a lovely one. A cheery hearth, children snug in their beds, and a husband reclining by her side, reading. Considering the pale-haired man next to her, she asked in confusion, "Wasn't there another in your place before?"

The man shook his head but remained engrossed in his book.

Wendy frowned. She seemed to remember a chestnut head and brilliant green eyes, both gone before she could get a fix on his elusive features. And a name... Not James but something infinitely dearer. Like a hint of jasmine on the wind, the memory embraced her and was gone.

"Perhaps not," she said faintly, squeezing herself as small as possible. She tried to sleep next to her husband, something inside her kept crying, "Woman, woman, let go of me."

DUKE YORK
Much Ado About Nothing

15

The Girl in the Park

*P*eter *stepped out of dimly-lit Victoria Station into the bright, busy street. This was London. Peter was sure he was in London, but to tell the truth, the surroundings looked more like New York. He couldn't be in America still—he had to get home! Wendy needed him.*

He started to run down the unfamiliar street, turning right or left by instinct at unrecognizable corners until he was quite lost. In desperation, he approached a passing stranger, a fine lady.

"Excuse me Miss, do you know the way to Highbuy Street?"

"Peter," the lady replied. "Do you not know me?"

He had met so many young ladies since taking the stage that he, indeed, could not remember them all, at least not well. With annoyance, he regarded the lovely stranger. "I'm sorry, Miss—" He was about to explain that he could not recall their acquaintance, when she somewhat impatiently interrupted him.

"I'm Wendy," she said agitatedly.

Peter gasped, looking at her and straining until there was the tiniest glimmer of recognition. "I'm very sorry, Wendy. I say," he whispered to her, "always if you see me forgetting you, just keep on saying 'I'm Wendy,' and then I'll remember."

For the rest of the dream as he kept passing her on unfamiliar streets, she would say 'I'm Wendy,' and he would remember. Each time he was bitterly sorry and silently vowed never to forget again, but the moment they parted, her memory faded. She was forgotten.

When Griffin suggested they take a walk through Kensington Gardens, Peter heartily agreed on account of the fine weather. Peter had always loved this particular park. It was one of the few things he missed while overseas. He was grateful for such a fine day to enjoy Kensington one last time.

Since his hasty return to London, his dreams had taken on a life of their own, a dark and troubling menace that clung to the edges of his reality. Although his brother was more the type to take stock in the subconscious, Peter did believe that these particular dreams carried a message. And with the message came action.

So without preamble he said, "I am returning to America, Griffin."

His brother frowned. "Without speaking to Miss Darling?"

"I have to let her go. She has a love—worships him, the undeserving sod—and she's blissfully happy. That's all matters."

"But Peter—"

"No." Peter interjected quite decidedly. "I must forget about her for my own sake, and especially for hers."

Griffin chuckled, "Aye, Peter. If you were able to accomplish that, you wouldn't have dropped everything and spent the last fortnight crossing an ocean to get home."

"I can at least try," Peter insisted. "Maybe with enough distance and distraction, I could accomplish it."

"So you are going to return to America, then? Find some measure of happiness in the embrace of an American lass?"

"Never, Griffin!" Peter cried passionately. "I gave my heart away to Wendy long ago. How should I every marry another without a heart?"

"Aye, that would pose a problem."

"Tell me then, what should I do?" His troubled eyes probed the other's in earnest for some advice, some respite to his hopeless predicament.

"Well," began his brother, "it seems to me that if you came all this way for her, you should at least see her."

"And then what?"

"Talk to her."

"And say what? Don't marry your fiancé, Miss Darling. Run away, instead, with me." He raked his hand through his hair in frustration.

Ignoring his brother's self-deprecating tone, Griffin nodded thoughtfully. "That would serve as an opening."

Peter continued his lament. "Run away from respectability to live the life of a vagabond. Forego the quiet joy of a banker's wife by wedding a socially inferior actor. No. I could never abuse her so."

"Socially inferior? Are not the best parlors of London open to Peter Neverland?"

"All the money in the world cannot afford one ounce of propriety." As this was said sharply, Griffin was taken aback by the cynicism evidenced in his brother's grave words and rendered momentarily speechless.

Peter squeezed his eyes shut and raked his fingers through his unruly hair. "For all I have heard, James Whitby III is the love of Wendy's life."

"James Whitby III," Griffin asked not altogether unamused. "You know your competition by name, then?"

Shuddering, Peter's hollow eyes turned inward. "He haunts my dreams, Griffin. I have never met this luckiest of men, but in my dreams, he is—*sinister*. He is a villain with the blackest of hearts and an iron claw for a hand. It is this loathsome blackguard to whom Wendy is betrothed. Even if he were the opposite of the personage that I have created him to be in my mind, he still could not deserve her. And yet, as she ardently loves him, he must be the most worthy of men."

Griffin could see that his brother was deeply troubled so he did not find fault. Instead, he looked off into the distance. "Maybe there is truth in dreams. While Mr. Whitby may not appear to be wicked, we cannot know the condition of his heart. Perhaps you are *meant* to save her."

"If only... Would it be very wrong of me to ask the heavens for a sign?"

"It could not hurt," the elder boy answered slyly. "Do it now Peter," he urged.

As Peter bowed his head in silent petition, his brother and confidant focused on the fine figure of an approaching lady. Although Peter had been too distracted to notice, Griffin had lived with his brother's obsession long enough to recognize Miss Wendy Moira Angela Darling by the merest of glances.

The day was fine. The air scented with blossoms and the breeze warm, hinting that summer was on its way. To Wendy the day was perfect, sunny and fragrant and oozing with—*freedom*!

The wedding was less than a week away. As her mother and Aunt Mildred argued about salmon and other reception delicacies, Wendy had escaped to the one place that held her eternal girlhood. She knew that Maimie would be at Kensington Gardens, along with her darling infant son and his red-cheeked nursemaid, taking in the fine spring weather. More than anything, Wendy longed for one last innocent stroll with her most bosom friend.

The next time she walked these enchanting paths, would she be Wendy Moira Angela Whitby, wife? And how long until she had her own nurse-maid in tow? She both longed and dreaded the day. In her mind's eye she could only picture chestnut-haired babes with penetrating emerald eyes...

She shook her head vigorously to dispel the vision. It was perfectly normal, she supposed, to have some lapse of nerves this close to the nuptial day. It did not, despite what Maimie had insinuated, have to do with the return of a certain actor, who no longer mattered to her in the slightest.

Wendy was steeling herself to argue with her friend that very point when she rounded a bend and collided, bodily, with the very subject of said point. Before she could draw a breath, she found herself in the steadying arms of Peter Neverland. Gasping, she reflexively stepped back, shrinking from what would certainly be misconstrued as an embrace. In her haste, she stumbled, causing Peter to spring forward and embrace her anew.

The fine weather had tempted most of London to pass the afternoon out of doors, and the commotion seemed to draw every eye and ear within hearing. Wendy colored, helpless as the blood pooled behind her pale cheeks. She could not help but imagine how the scene must appear to curious onlookers. To make matters worse, Peter's own brother stood off to one side, a shrewd enigmatic smile on his face.

"Miss Darling!" Peter exclaimed looking shocked and still holding her about the waist. "Forgive me for the impropriety, but I must speak with you. We met some time ago. My name is Peter Neverland."

Blushing and flustered, Wendy kept her eyes on her shoes. "I know who you are, Sir."

She could hear a crowd gathering around them now. How many of the spectators knew who she was? Surely some recognized her as the fiancée of James Whitby III. How many more must recognize Peter?

She couldn't seem to take in enough air. Despite the layers of clothing, Peter's hands burned where they rested upon her. Her face felt hot, and she suspected she was about to faint.

If she fainted, Peter would have no choice but to scoop her into his arms and cradle her against his chest. How would she ever explain that? She would bring shame on her family, on James. The humiliation enhanced her lightheadedness. Tear stung her eyes, threatening to gush. She wrenched herself from Peter's steadying hands. Blindly, Wendy turned to flee.

"Wait!" Heedless of propriety, Peter reached for her.

She felt him grasp her shawl. Without stopping, Wendy jerked forward, pleading, "Please, please leave me be!"

Painfully aware of the instant that Peter let her go, Wendy ran to the far end of the park, where there was an oft-overlooked path and a very private bench. It was there, on that out-of-the-way bench, that Maimie found her sobbing her eyes out.

"Dearest," exclaimed her friend, coming to sit beside her. "I thought I might find you here. Are you all right? I heard you were accosted."

The misinformation brought Wendy up short. "Accosted, dear Maimie? No." She wiped at her eyes trying to make less of the encounter—surely in the retelling, it would not seem like the cataclysmic event that Wendy had made it out to be. "Not accosted. I bumped into a gentleman is all. I lost my footing, and he helped me regain it."

"Who was the gentleman?"

Wendy ducked her head. "No one."

Sagely, Maimie nodded. "Of course. When *I* bump into 'no one,' I often hide myself away and sob. That is perfectly understandable behavior."

The sarcasm only served to start Wendy crying anew. Unable to stand by while her dearest friend wept, Maimie went to great lengths to make amends. When she finally had Wendy calmed down, she gently asked, "What is it really? Is it wedding jitters—because that is perfectly normal. Remember my antics, like trying to join that convent?"

While Wendy appreciated her friend's attempt to distract her, she was in no humour for levity. "It is not jitters, exactly. The 'no one' I ran into was the very *someone* I was seeking to avoid."

Maimie's sharp intake of breath, confirmed that the girl knew her better than anyone. "No! Peter was here?"

"Yes," Wendy said miserably, "I bumped into him. Then stammered and staggered so that I drew a crowd. He tried to speak with me, and I panicked. Why do I turn into a perfect disaster every time he comes near?"

"Love?"

Although her friend's response was sympathetic, there was an underlying shrewdness that pierced Wendy. "After all this time, how could I still love him?"

Maimie shrugged prettily, adding, "Maybe he loves you, too."

"You are insane," cried Wendy. "Quite mad if you are suggesting that Peter Neverland loves me."

"Really?" The girl arched an artful brow. "What did Peter say to you exactly?"

"He said, 'Miss Darling forgive the impropriety, but I have to speak to you.'"

"And then?"

Wendy knit her brows in consternation. "And then I thought I was going to faint—so, I ran away."

With a most severe look, Maimie continued, "Nothing else was said between you?"

Wendy looked mournfully at her shoes. "I might have begged him to leave me be..."

Maimie let Wendy stew in her thoughts a few moments before asking, "Is that what you want? Truly?"

Leaping from the bench, Wendy began to pace. "It is not about what I want. It's for the best. I marry James in a week. This is not something that I am entering into unwillingly. I warmed to him. I encouraged him. And when he proposed I accepted him. I have a duty to him."

"And what of love? What if bumping into Peter was a sign? Can Juliet truly be happy with Paris? Especially when Romeo is within her grasp?"

"Juliet is going to do her best," Wendy stated grimly. With a sigh, she shook her head at her friend's romantic folly. "I do not have the luxury of believing in signs, not when I am bound by duty." Maimie opened her mouth but Wendy silenced her by saying, "No, we shan't talk of Peter again. It is best if I just forget him."

The brave Wendy and the arrogant Peter would have been shocked by the cowardice and doubt that plagued their adult selves. They would have sorely reprimanded their grown-up counterparts, that is, if they'd not been so deeply buried, they'd lost any say in the matter. As it were, all their inner child could do was to whisper accusingly, "You have forgotten the way!"

Peter held her fast to the rock, his body covering hers, buffeting her from the fierce waves that pounded them. Again and again, his manly form smashed against her, and in spite of the dire circumstances, her body thrilled in response to him.

Something tickled her cheek, as soft as a kiss, but for the life of her, she couldn't think what it was. Peter grasped at it. "Salvation!" he exclaimed, almost brightly. She looked to see a cheerful little kite, dancing on the wind, as if to say, "Can I be of assistance?"

Wendy looked from Peter to the little kite and back, her heart sinking. "I fear it cannot carry the both of us."

"It won't have to." Already, he had tied the tail round her waist.

"Peter," she protested, clinging to his neck, "I shan't go without you."

"You must, Wendy. The rock is growing smaller. Soon the water will be over it!"

"I won't leave you to die alone."

"Better than both of us dying, my love."

Like a petulant child she stuck out her lower lip, stubbornly proclaiming, "I'll not leave you."

Peter disengaged himself from her grasp. "I'm sorry, Wendy. I have to let you go."

"No Peter, please!"

"Good-bye, Wendy." Peter pushed her away from him, and she began to rise with the little kite. Despite struggling to get back to him, it was no use. In a few minutes, she was borne from his sight, and Peter was left alone to die.

Wendy woke with a gasp, a fine sheen of sweat covering her face, her bedsheet tangled about her waist. The dream troubled her greatly. Was it saying that she had to let go or that she should not? The more she tried to focus on the details the more muddled they became, yet deciphering the meaning seemed of vital importance. The clock was ticking... With a shudder she realized that she had less than a week to figure it out.

16

Come Away, Come Away!

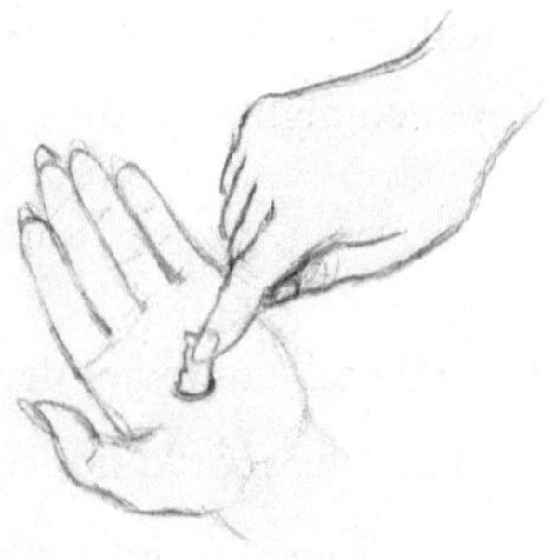

Peter ran through the thick forest toward a little earthen house where Wendy slept. The pirates could be heard carousing far away, and the wolves were on the prowl. He drew his sword, determined to stand guard and keep her safe. As he approached the house, he realized that the door was asunder. Then the song of the pirates grew louder, and Peter instantly knew the reason. The thought of Wendy bound and on the pirate ship caused his heart to bob up and down.

"I'll rescue her!" he cried. "Hook or me this time."

Peter stood outside No. 14, watching from the stillness of the garden. In one corner stood an ancient doghouse, the name Nana carved across the top. It was in such a forlorn condition that Peter felt satisfied its occupant was long gone from this earth. So he scaled the iron gate.

He still wasn't sure what he was doing. Surely, the hook-handed pirate captain from his nightmares was not waiting in the shadows to kidnap Wendy. But the sentiments behind his dream had seemed so real that he couldn't quite talk himself out of the idea that Wendy needed saving. He couldn't shake the feeling that she was in grave danger, so he had come to reassure himself that she was safe.

Winding though the shadows, Peter made his way to the trellis that had tempted him on many such nights. At the top was the one thing he loved most in the world.

"Peter, oh Peter..."

He stilled as he heard Wendy call out in her sleep. Surely, his ears were playing tricks on him. He knew he should not continue and, for a moment, hesitated in indecision. *If she calls my name again*, he thought, *I will go to her*. As if privy to his hopes, Wendy softly murmured, *"Peter..."* And the decision was made.

Quietly, climbing her trellis, Peter felt like the most heartless thing in the world, entirely selfish. He knew he should halt, but the thought of seeing her was too tempting to resist. So clearly could he picture her slumbering, that it seemed as if he had spied on her before.

When he reached the top, his heart began to boom in his chest. Trembling, he knew he was looking through the open window at the one joy from which he must be forever barred.

There could not have been a lovelier sight; bathed in moonlight, Wendy was safely asleep in her four-poster bed. Her sweet mouth was drawn in such a way that her innermost kiss mocked him.

Suddenly, he longed to give her something of himself, a final gift. Slipping into the room, he approached the bed. His hand crept into his pocket and pulled out his good luck charm. It seemed right to Peter the thing he loved second best in the entire world should belong to the first.

Wendy stirred in her sleep, and Peter dropped to the floor in a panic. He knew he should go. The impropriety of his actions was shameful. What if she wakened to find him in her chamber? Surely, she would detest him more than she already did!

No. Wendy could never know that he had been here. Still as much as he was ashamed for his conduct, he felt worse about leaving. How could he leave his very self? The pain of separation had weighed so heavily on him the first time that he did not think he could survive it again! Was this to be the last time he laid eyes on his Wendy?

If only she would wake up. There was so much he wanted to say to her—so much that was in his heart. Even if she rejected him, as she no doubt would, at least she would know his feelings.

From somewhere below a clock chimed reminding Peter that he could not tarry. He then uttered what was undoubtedly the most painful word in the English language. "Goodbye."

He was creeping slowing back toward the window when Wendy sat straight up in her bed. She did not seem alarmed to see a stranger on her bedroom floor, only pleasantly interested.

"Boy," she asked courteously, "why are you crying?"

Astonished, Peter raised his hand to his cheek and felt its dampness. He *had* been crying, only without realizing it.

Before he could speak, Wendy continued. "It must be sewn on," she said, just a little patronizingly.

Peter was at a complete loss, until he realized that Wendy's conversation was not with him—not really. Her pale eyes had the glaze of one still dreaming. Yet in spite of her dream-like state, the conversation felt to him entirely personal, and he wondered at it.

Still in slumber, Wendy stood and crossed to the open window reaching with her hand. "Don't go, Peter," she entreated. "I know such lots of stories."

Peter watched with shock as she climbed the window ledge, exclaiming, "Oh, how lovely to fly." As she reached out into the abyss of night, Peter grabbed her from behind and pulled her roughly back into the room. Her body slammed against his as he held her fast.

Wendy gasped, and her eyes cleared. She looked around in a daze. Then realizing she was pressed against the hard form of a man, she began to struggle.

"Let me go!" she ordered him.

Shocked, Peter released his hold on her.

As she swung around, Wendy's eyes widened in recognition. "You!" she gasped. "Will you never give me any peace? Just go away!"

The absolute folly of his behavior became clear as she confronted him. He was such a fool! "I'm sorry," he muttered as he launched himself out the window. He did not look back as he rapidly climbed down the trellis, ran across the garden and vaulted over the gate. Indeed, he did not look back until he was two streets over.

If he had had any doubts concerning Wendy's sentiments toward him, he harbored them no longer. She despised him. And tomorrow—tomorrow she would pledge herself to another, and his heartbreak would be complete.

Peter's sole consolation was that he could most likely make the morning train before the constable could track him down and bring scandal upon his respectable brother. As he hurried home to pack, it seemed the very wind was calling out to him, mocking him in Wendy's melodious voice. *Peter!* it called. *Peter, come back!*

Wendy closed her eyes and focused on mastering her breathing. Her heart was racing. She had been moving about in her sleep again, her dreams so vivid that she was having trouble shaking them off. She had not merely dreamt Peter this time—she had *felt* him. She had felt the warmth of his body as he clasped her to him, heard his irresistible voice apologizing, and saw the well of agony in his exquisite green eyes. He had been so real! However, she had seen him at the foot of her bed so often in her dreams that she thought this was just the dream hanging around her still.

It was the dream Peter she had reacted to with her uncharitable comments. And rightly so. The dream Peter deserved to be chastised for tormenting her on a nightly basis. Had she realized this Peter was no apparition, she would have spoken only kindness to him, despite the impropriety of their circumstances.

Slowly crossing to the open window, Wendy searched for any trace that Peter had actually been in her room. She examined the deep shadows of the garden and then scrutinized the starry sky. But with a single exception of a barking dog on the next street over, the night was still. Heaving a sigh of disappointment, she turned away from the window, forcing herself to remember every detail of the dream.

"Peter held me here," she murmured moving about the room. "I twisted away, here. Then..." she hesitated. In her dream, he had gripped her arms so tightly. Absently, she touched the spot where his hand had branded her upper arm, then pulled it away surprised at the tenderness of the flesh. Hastily pushing up her sleeve, she examined first one arm then the other. Her breath came faster as she realized both arms were marked with large finger-like bruises just below the shoulder. Peter had held her! She was not crazy, and she was not dreaming—she had been in his arms this very night! Hurrying to the window, Wendy thrust her head out calling for him at the top of her lungs.

"Peter!" she yelled. "Peter, come back!"

She only stopped when the street below began stir. Not wanting to explain herself to the constable, she retreated. It was then that Wendy's attention turned to the tiny trinket lying forlorn on her bedroom floor. With a frown, she bent to scoop up the object. It was her dear little thimble half. How had it gotten on the floor? She had not looked at it in months. With a start, she wondered if Peter had taken it out of her treasure box. Had he wanted it? Had he realized how much it meant to her? Still if he had but asked, she would have gladly given it to him. Didn't he know that? Couldn't he feel it? She would have given Peter anything; all he had to do was ask her.

More puzzling to her than why he had come, was why had he run away?

Then she recalled less than a week hence, she had begged him to leave her be. Oh, how she wished with all her soul she could take those horrid words back. If she could but go back in time, she would confess to him her every secret hope and beg him to hold her as he had tonight.

Clutching the thimble half to her breast, Wendy laid back down in her bed, feeling as if her dreams had turned to waking nightmares and doubting if she would ever be able to sleep again. Just before dawn, however, she slipped into a fitful, treacherous slumber.

The aisle was so long, and the white dress so heavy. She wanted to stop and rest. Far ahead, she saw James waiting for her. He had been so patient and kind that she could not bear to disappoint him. She saw her parents' expectant faces. They looked so proud of her. And her brothers smiled. Even

grim Aunt Mildred seemed to approve that she was doing her duty. She didn't want to disappoint any of them so she kept moving forward.

When she reached the altar, James was facing away from her. Gently she touched his hand to declare her arrival. James turned then. As he did so, his blonde hair darkened to pitch and wound about his shoulders in long curls. His suit transformed, turning into velvet and lace that ridiculously aped the style of Charles II. Then his cadaverous face looked down upon her and his eyes—the blue of the forget-me-nots—fixed on her as two malignant red spots appeared in them. He had a singularly threatening expression to his handsome countenance indicative of a black heart. However, the grimmest part was the hand that connected her to James no longer gripped flesh and blood but an iron claw.

"At last, Wendy," James said darkly, "you are mine."

There are no words to tell how Wendy despised him at that moment. She fought to free herself, but she was outmatched. James's good hand clamped bitingly into her waist, while the odious hook scratched along the bodice of her gown menacingly. "I have waited a long time for you," he sneered, his black voice full of vindictiveness.

"Please," she begged. In a panic, she shut her eyes to the monster that was her husband-to-be. "Please!" she pleaded.

"Wendy, come!"

The voice that cried imperiously to her came straight from the Heavens. She opened her eyes and saw Peter standing at the far end of the aisle beckoning to her. In that instant, she believed with all her heart, she was rescued, until she felt the cruel tip of James's claw prick her breastbone.

"Peter!" She barely had time to call out before the hook pierced her heart and silenced her hopes forever.

17

The Riddle of Existence

H*ook!*

Wendy bolted straight up in bed clutching at her chest. The dream had been so real that the shadow of pain lingered even after waking. She gasped as her hand came away from her breast wet and red. Looking down, she examined the bloom of a scarlet flower on the bodice of her white nightgown. With a rising panic, she struggled to get the garment off, fearing what she would find underneath.

Instead of the fatal wound from her dreams, there was a long superficial scratch diagonally across her heart. Frowning she traced the length of the injury with her finger. Surely it had been self-inflected...hadn't it?

As she moved to don her dressing gown, she became aware of the little thimble half still clenched in her hand. The thimble recalled to her the strange events of the previous night—Peter's mysterious visit and even more puzzling exit. Again, she wondered what had brought him to her bedchamber in the middle of the night. If there were only some way to make a respectable inquiry after him—however, there was not a bit of propriety to be found in asking after another man mere hours before she was to be wed.

The sound of Maimie's motorcar in the street below roused Wendy from her scheming. She reminded herself of her pledge to put away childish things, in both the literal and figurative senses, and hurried to her treasure box. She would return to the box her dear thimble and place right alongside it her girlish fancy for Peter Neverland. Then she would shut the box and embrace her duty.

This was how Maimie found Wendy. Standing over her treasure box in her dressing gown, mouth agape, gravely pale, and holding a tiny porcelain thimble half in each hand.

"Dearest," Maimie exclaimed as she hastened to her friend's side, "are you ill?"

Wendy slowly shook her head back and forth.

"Scared? Oh, don't worry, Wendy. It will soon be over. Marriage isn't all bad, and I have prepared you for your wedding night, which is more than was done for me. Call Old Liza, and we shall start the preparations. Look, I brought quite a lovely blue garter for you to borrow—" The merry young lady paused at Wendy's lack of response. Then inspecting her friend more closely, she grasped the significance of the thimble pieces.

"Isn't that your mysterious sixteenth birthday present? Where on earth did you find the other half?"

Wendy shivered, whispering in an almost inaudible voice, "Peter."

"What?" Maimie grabbed Wendy's shoulders and turned her around to better question her. "What do you mean Peter?"

Still grave, Wendy met her friend's narrowed eyes with her huge unblinking ones. Holding out her left hand, she explained, "Peter left this for me. I suspect he's had it all along."

"Where did he leave it?"

"Here. In my room."

Maimie gasped at the shocking revelation. "Peter was in *your* bedroom? When?"

"Last night—or early this morning—I am not sure. I thought I was dreaming again. I yelled at him, and he fled. He left this behind." Wendy sank to the floor cradling both trinket halves. "Oh, Maimie, I drove him away again. I didn't let him explain. Now I have no idea what he wanted or why he came or what *this* means." She held up the thimble in resignation.

Deep in concentration, Maimie held out her hands for the thimble halves. Wendy watched as Maimie frowned first over one, then the other, and then finally held them together. They were a perfect fit. "Call Liza!" she whispered excitedly. "You will need some writing paper and glue right away!"

Wendy felt slightly annoyed at the agitation in her friend's demeanor. After all, she was just hours from her wedding and had every right to expect Maimie to be the calm voice of reason amidst the insanity. "Why?" she asked.

"Because, dearest, you are going to write a letter to Peter, straightaway."

"What is the use, Maimie? To torment him? Or give myself false hopes? You said yourself all will be over soon. Today I am to be married."

"Over my dead body!" Maimie vehemently cried. "For someone with a proclivity for the poetic, you are being frustratingly obtuse. Don't you see it?" She held up the thimble half in her right hand. "This, Wendy, is you—ragged, incomplete, useless—and this," she raised her left hand and the other thimble piece, "this is Peter. *He* is your other half! Together you are whole and beautiful!"

Despite the improbability of Maimie's words, Wendy trembled with hope as their truth resonated deep inside her heart. "What if it is too late?"

"It cannot be. Don't you see Wendy? I need to believe! I desperately need to clap my hands together and believe that love does not die. You have a chance at true bliss and you have to try for it! For all of us!"

Wendy squeezed her eyes shut and pressed her lip together as she tried to make her choice. As torn as she was between her obligation and her secret hopes, she was most afraid that upon giving in to those hopes, they would be sorely disappointed. Then she would have sacrificed her obligation for nothing. Could she risk her heart and her world for Maimie, for Peter, most of all, for herself? With a terse nod, she made her decision. "Send for the writing paper and glue, Maimie. I shall send Peter an olive branch. And then I shall prepare for my duty."

Tick, tick, tick, tick.

The sound was steady at first.

Tick, tick, tick, tick.

Then the noise began to stutter.

Tick...t-tick...t-ti-ck

Like a clock running down and coming to a halt, it stopped. He could no longer hear it coming. Peter was filled with dread then. Something was about to get them—something predatory and silent. No more warning. And time was running out...

Peter awkwardly awoke on the bench in Victoria Station with the most acute sense of foreboding. He hadn't meant to doze, much less dream. In actuality, dreaming would have been a relief; the relentless nightmares that visited him instead were terrifying.

Still smarting from the night's folly, he had crept home like a thief in the night to pack his bag and pen a quick letter to Griffin. Then he had slunk off to the railway station to hide and await the morning train to Wales. Sometime near daybreak, he must have drifted off to sleep.

This is how Griffin found Peter. Stomach in knots, slumped over on a bench with his head in his hands. Fear for Wendy's safety blanketing his body in a cold sweat.

"Peter," Griffin gasped. Out of breath from running, he was unable to say more.

"I'm sorry Griffin," Peter said instantly chagrined. "I did something foolish, and I snuck away in the middle of the night because I was embarrassed to face you. Can you forgive me?"

"No, Peter—" Griffin paused again to raggedly draw in air.

Misunderstanding his brother's haste, Peter answered, "I don't blame you, brother. There is nothing that can excuse how badly I have behaved. It is better for all if I just go."

"No, Peter." Griffin held out a small package. "This—came—for—you."

Peter took the package from his brother frowning at his name scrawled across the front in elegant script. He was used to the admiration of females and the lavish gifts they would sometimes send to gain his notice, but his brother, understandably, was not. "Griffin, really. You came all the way here for this?"

"I came—for you—Peter. The messenger said—it was—from—Miss—Wendy Darling."

Peter froze. His eyes were huge, and his hands trembled slightly as he slowly opened the parcel. Inside was an envelope and a small object in wrapping tissue. As he opened the letter and read the few lines, his face turned white as a sheet. Then he edged open the tissue with a soft groan. His eyes conveyed the agony of a thousand tragedies as he held the object out for his brother to examine.

Peter saw the recognition on his brother's face. "Your talisman—restored—what does it mean Peter?"

"Don't you see Griffin? She is my other half. Wendy is the riddle of my existence!"

Just then, a clock chimed, startling Peter and recalling to him his nightmare. *Time is running out*, he thought. He remembered Wendy was to be married. "I have to get to Wendy! Do you know from which church she marries today?"

"Aye Peter, but we may already be too late."

"No." He shook his head back and forth, his jaw hard set in determination. Something about the talisman made whole allowed the arrogant Peter of old to reunite with his more mature doubt-riddled self. Peter's lost boy, now resurfaced, gave him the confidence needed to pursue a single and reckless course of action. "If I have to, I will forbid the banns."

"Peter." His brother took him by the shoulders to better face him. "Don't be rash. Think of Wendy's place in society. It will not do for you to make a scene—for you or her."

Peter waved the thimble at him. "I *have* to believe we are meant for happiness in this life—that we are destined to find our other half and be made whole. Don't you see brother? I have to *believe*!" His words, so genuine and spoken with such passion, swayed the elder brother instantly.

"Come on then," Griffin replied. "We must hurry."

"No, Griffin," Peter cried breaking into a full-fledged run. "We have to fly!"

18

The Neverland Breaks Through

If Peter comes and gives me a kiss, I will not go through with it!

This is what Wendy told Maimie in her bedroom then repeated to herself only minutes before her father had walked her down the aisle. She repeated it again now—like a mantra.

The hideous nightmare from the previous night—the one where James turned into the horrible hook-handed pirate captain, the one where he claimed her as his own despite her protests—seemed to be a bad omen. However, she had also had the other dream—the lovely one with boy, her salvation, in her room beckoning...*Come away, come away!*

She pinched herself to be sure she was not dreaming still. Dressed in white with a pink sash, standing most solemnly atop the holy altar, the sharp pain inflicted by her own hand convinced her that the wedding was, indeed, happening.

How she wished she were still in her bed!

She thought of the thimble halves again. What had they been trying to tell her? At Maimie's urging, she had repentantly glued the halves together and sent them by messenger back to Peter with a note that simply said, *you will always have my heart!* Her olive branch. James might have her obligation, her duty, but the keeping of her heart she entrusted to Peter alone.

While the vicar spoke most eloquently, extolling the virtues of marriage, Wendy made a miserable attempt of convincing herself that marriage to James was her first choice and was, indeed, something she wanted. She had tried to grow up, to make the correct decisions and appease those around her. But when she examined her heart, the tiny seed of Peter that had taken residence there was impossible to uproot. It would always live inside of her, sheltered and waiting to blossom with the merest of encouragement.

A slight commotion at the back of the chapel caught Wendy's straying attention. As she turned to look, hope began thumping wildly in her chest. At the far end of the aisle stood a solemn, vaguely familiar looking dark-haired man and coming purposefully down the aisle, his burning emerald eyes fastened on her, was Peter Neverland.

She felt her throat tighten and the color rise to her cheeks. So far, he had escaped the notice of the congregation, but as he approached the front, she knew for certain that would change. *Guide me*, she prayed not to God or the Heavens but to her inner self.

Wendy fought to control the blush that threatened to engulf her. What should she do? She had her family to think of, her duty as a daughter, and her obligation to society.

Halfway down the aisle Aunt Mildred stood, inserting herself between Peter and the ceremony at front. They exchanged words in low tones. Anger at the old woman's interference caused Wendy to burn. How dare the old woman presume to speak to him on her behalf?

Act Wendy!

The voice was at first low, then growing in pitch and urgency from deep inside of her until it would not be ignored. *Act!* In a last desperate attempt, the brave Wendy was trying to make herself heard. Suddenly desperate to hear what was being said, it became more important to Wendy than any impropriety on her part and before she knew it, her choice was made.

Slowing moving up the aisle toward her heart's desire, she stopped just short of her meddlesome aunt. "Aunt Mildred?" she inquired.

"Wendy," the old woman gasped. "Really you shouldn't have troubled yourself. The boy just wanted to give you a wedding gift. Go back to James," she hissed quietly. "I will take care of it for you."

But with the brave Wendy at her side, she didn't budge. "I think you have taken care of quite enough. Please stand aside so that I can hear what Mr. Neverland has come to say."

Knowing all eyes were on her, Wendy glared until the old woman retreated with a fish-like frown. Then, there was only Peter, standing in front of her, his intense eyes boring two holes into her soul. He looked at her expectantly.

Wendy felt the color in her cheeks deepen and spread under his agonizing stare. She looked down. "You have a gift for me?" she asked shyly, dipping her head.

"A thimble," Peter said gravely holding out his hand to show her the recently restored porcelain trinket. "Now shall I give it to you?"

"If you wish to," said Wendy keeping her head erect this time.

Peter stepped forward to close the gap between them. His one hand held out the gift while the other brushed her hip on its way to the small of her back so that he could pull her close to him.

Peter thimbled her.

Never in history was there a sweeter, tenderer "thimble." The caress of his lips across hers was electric. Her mouth began to dance with his, and she opened to him without thinking. He deepened their kiss, and the chapel with all of its onlookers disappeared as the Neverland broke through. In all truth, the island was looking for them as a million golden arrows flashed pointing the way. Not at all like a dream, details came rushing back with certain clarity as adventure quickened their veins.

At once Wendy recalled who Peter was and what she had once been to him.

Wendy's mouth was full of thimbles. As Peter took every one of them, the Neverland again woke into life. The seething island came surging back in vivid images. He knew it all then, the lagoon, Hook, the lost boys, Tink and most of all his own Wendy. Taking her sweet face between his hands, he murmured, "My Wendy—my own."

Her surprised eyes fastened on his, and he knew his Wendy remembered him as well. "Oh, Peter!" she exclaimed. "You've come back!"

His finger traced a line down the tip of her nose. "You've forgotten how to fly," he admonished.

"And you, Peter—" She ran her fingers along the shadow of his jaw feeling the stubble of his whiskers. "You've become a man."

His chest thumped as he remembered that fateful night in the garden.

"You promised me you wouldn't grow up."

"I couldn't help it." She was smiling at it all, but they were wet smiles.

Giving a single anguished nod, Peter pressed his lips together, confessing, "I became a man because of you, Wendy."

Her eyes widened, and she gasped with feeling at some recrimination he did not intend. "No, Peter!"

"Shhh, dearest," he soothed, caressing her downy cheek. "I wanted to grow up—to become a man for you. You are my own... I love you, Wendy."

"I love you, too, Peter. I always have."

The conversation would have continued as such except for a peculiar noise that cut through the moment. Clearing his throat, Mr. Darling stood behind them looking quite cross. At his side, although not quite so formidable, stood his lovely wife, Mrs. Darling.

As Wendy turned to face them, Peter's hands moved to encircle her waist in a protective embrace. "Mother, Father," she said looking from one to the other. "This is Peter."

Mr. Darling was red-faced. "Now see here—" he upbraided.

Mrs. Darling, however, stayed her husband with a gentle hand on his forearm. There was something in the right-hand corner of her mouth that wanted her not to call Peter names. "You're Peter?" she asked in surprise.

Wendy nodded happily. "You see, I gave my heart to Peter so long ago that I had quite forgotten about it until this very moment. I am terribly sorry, but I simply cannot marry James."

Mr. Darling wanted to say something about that and would have, had not his clever wife intervened on the lovers' behalf. "How romantic. George dear," she remarked to her husband. Then, although it bore no resemblance, she observed, "It reminds me of the story of you and I.

Surely you would not begrudge your only daughter the same happiness that we have known."

Mrs. Darling's skill of stroking her husband's vanity and wrapping him around her little finger at the same time had only sharpened throughout their married life. She now played Mr. Darling like a virtuoso. Not wanting to offend his wife's romantic sensibilities, he replied, "Not at all, my dear. Not at all." He then offered his hand to Peter in a magnanimous gesture.

But what of Wendy's husband to be? Where was the intended groom during these surprising developments?

James Christopher Whitby III waited at the altar for the others to decide his fate. Being of blue blood, he was incapable of showing bad form, so rather than cause a scene, he placidly waited, taking comfort in the thought that what was meant to happen would come to pass. When the dashing young stranger approached holding Wendy fast to his side, he stiffened his upper lip in anticipation. The stranger then said something terribly smart about destiny and true love and James could not help but agree.

With a nod he turned to regard his almost bride-to-be, his eyes soft as periwinkle. "Of course," he muttered. "I see it now. That part of Wendy that I was missing. No matter how hard I tried, I couldn't capture it. Now I understand that it was never meant for me."

Then showing the very pinnacle of good form, James released Wendy of her obligation and wishing the couple well, took his leave with relatives in tow.

Mr. Darling, being an economical sort of fellow, remarked how it would be a shame to waste a perfectly good wedding which he had already expensed. So, with great joy and the slightest pretense of coercion, Peter and Wendy were married that same hour. Griffin cheered;

Maimie wept; and even disagreeable Aunt Mildred, presumably to save face, toasted the couple's good health.

Just like the thimble restored, Peter and Wendy slumbered that night as husband and wife, complete in each other's embrace. Together at last in their dreams, they danced through the Neverland surrounded by the twinkling of a thousand fairies. They were a perfect fit and pen cannot adequately describe the happy scene, over which we now draw a veil.

19

An Awfully Big Adventure

On the night of the funeral, Wendy entered the nursery for the very last time. The day had been long and weary with people coming and going, expressing condolences in hushed tones. Lord Peter Neverland had been much loved, and never was this more evident than by the current gathering of his friends and family.

Weeks earlier, Lady Wendy Neverland had made peace with the circumstances that were to bring about her husband's demise. She and Peter had led a most remarkable life, taking them across six continents. Happily, they had grown old together. And at the very end, they were as much in love as ever.

So that evening when she could bear no more weeping, Wendy deftly slipped from the cluster of mourners and into her old nursery.

Awaiting her arrival with notable anticipation were her descendants, her grands and great-grands. There were twelve of them in all, ranging in age from four to sixteen. Wendy greeted each child fondly. Then she settled herself by the hearth and pulled from her pocket a small chapter book of adventures, of which she was not only the storyteller but also the author.

"Now my darlings, which story shall you hear tonight?"

"Peter Pan and Hook!" cried little Peter.

"With the Indians," added the twins, John and Michael.

"And Wendy, Grandmama. Don't forget Wendy," exclaimed a tow-headed girl referring proudly to her namesake.

To the delight of the children, Lady Neverland opened the well-worn volume and began to read. She hardly had to look at the pages for she knew the story by heart.

Later that night, in the stillness of her own room, Lady Neverland took out the black oriental box that was still the keeper of her treasures. She carefully clasped the chain with the acorn button around her neck so that it rested against her breast. Then she paused to cherish each thimble before slipping them, one by one, into the pocket of her nightdress. The last thimble was most remarkable, a hand painted scene of an island surrounded by a turbulent sea, dotted with mermaids and containing a large pirate ship. It had appeared, without explanation, on her windowsill that very morning.

Reverently, she placed it in her pocket with the others. Then Wendy unfastened her hair, letting her white locks fall loose and wild about her shoulders. Crossing deliberately to the window, she opened it and peered into the twinkling midnight sky.

As the clock chimed, Wendy heard in the distance the most happiest of sounds, crowing. Soon she would be beckoned by the loveliest of phrases. *Come Away!*

And she was ready to go...

Earlier in the nursery, when the story had been read and the children were satisfied that Captain Hook had gotten his due, Lady Neverland herself had tucked each child into bed. She had tarried with loving care as if performing this duty for the last time.

"Where is Peter now, Grandmama?" Michael asked.

"He has returned to the Neverland to begin his final big adventure."

"Is Wendy with him?" inquired John.

"Not yet, my darlings, not yet. However, this very night Peter will make a final journey through the starry London sky. He will alight on Wendy's windowsill, sprinkle her with pixie dust, and together they will fly back to the Neverland where they shall live forever."

"Happy ever after!" exclaimed little Wendy.

"Yes, my angel. Forever and ever—happily ever after!"

THE END

Acknowledgements

Thank you to Elaine English and Naomi Hackenberg who loved this project from the beginning, to Lorie Langdon who has loved it all along, and AJ whose newfound love gives it a second chance. And to my project muse, Mr. J.M. Barrie, whose voice narrated softly in my ear to guide me on this amazing journey.

20

J. M. Barrie's World

Historical & Fictional Characters & Settings from J.M. Barrie's World

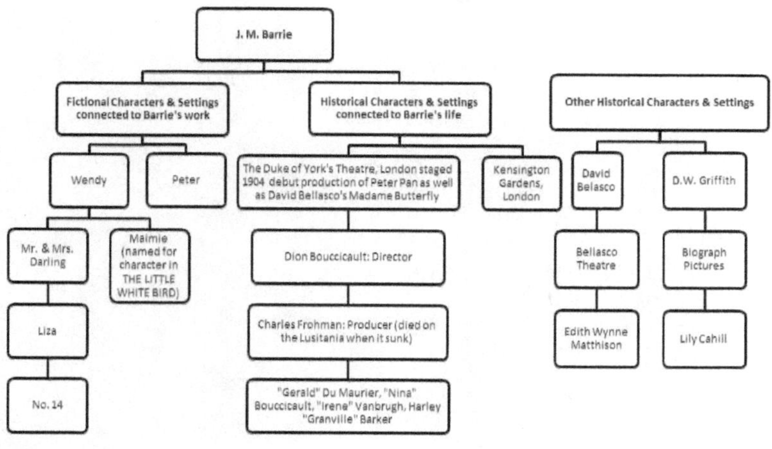

21

Discussion Guide

SHADES OF NEVERLAND - **Discussion Guide**

(Let your inner child guide you as you customize for your unique group)

1. What does the title: *Shades of Neverland* mean to you?

2. The book opens with a quote from J.M. Barrie's original work, *Peter Pan*. How do you feel this set the tone for the book?

3. Different types of romantic love are portrayed through the relationships Peter and Wendy experience, such as: Peter and the Tiger Lily; Wendy and James; Mr. and Mrs. Darling; Maimie and Viscount Withington; Peter and Wendy. Which relationship resonated the most with you and why? Which one resonated the least?

4. The author often takes a familiar phrase or concept from Barrie's original and weaves it into something new, for example the juxtaposition of thimbles and kisses. Can you think of an example in the story to share with the group?

5. What role does the theatre play in the lives of Wendy and Peter? Share with the group a hobby you are passionate about.

6. In the exploration of what it means to grow up, the author often contrasts childhood with adulthood. Which qualities are attributed to childhood? Which qualities are attributed to adulthood?

7. Most of the secondary characters Peter encounters in the London and New York theatre world and in Hollywood are historical. Choose one of particular interest to you and discuss.

8. The author frequently uses authorial intrusion to speak directly to the reader. Share an example of this. How does this enhance the overall effect of the story?

9. The Neverlands are written as a character of its own. What role do the Neverlands play in this book?

10. Discuss Peter's and Wendy's main strengths and weaknesses. How do their weaknesses contribute to their unhappiness?

11. Were there any scenes in *Shades of Neverland* that made you want to cheer? Cry? Reflect on your own life? What was your favorite scene?

12. Identify a trait from childhood that either Peter or Wendy sacrificed in order to grow up. Do you think that trait would have been beneficial to them in adulthood? Describe one of your best qualities from childhood. Do you still possess that quality? How much of a role does this quality play in your everyday life?

13. As Wendy grows up, more and more of her life becomes focused on her obligations. Are those obligations to herself or to others? Give some examples. If you could be free of all obligations, how

would your life be different?

14. Through Peter Pan, J.M. Barrie says, "To die will be an awfully big adventure." What does this mean to you? How does this relate to the final chapter?

15. In the Author's note, Carey Corp writes, "This is a story about lost selves." Describe a time that you felt lost or disconnected from the person you used to be.

16. "When you fearlessly follow your inner child with hope, trust and a dash of pixie dust, all things are possible." What does this mean to you in the context of the story? What does this mean in the context of your own life?

17. What advice would you share with a young person about growing up?